Bed, Breakfast, and Murder

by

Scott Sowers

DEDICATION

This book is dedicated to dogs everywhere and the humans who love them.

A Big Gorilla Press Production – 2019
Revised Edition 2020
Re-Revised Edition 2023

A Blurb

Fast-paced and cleverly plotted, "Bed, Breakfast, and Murder" features a well-defined cast of characters, lively dialogue, and refreshing interludes where we watch the action from Mooky's point of view. – *Karen Lyon, Literary Editor, The Hill Rag*

Acknowledgements

I would like to acknowledge the support and forward momentum provided by participating in the Novels in Progress Group in Washington, D.C. Everybody works better with a deadline.

Bed, Breakfast, and Murder

Chapter 1

Mooky lay in the kitchen where she had a view of the front and the back door; she knew Vivien was going away, and Mooky wanted to go too. She knew this was a trip that might last a long time because Vivien had clothes all over the bed and the suitcase was in the hallway. Getting to go would be the most wonderful thing in the world. As Vivien walked by whistling to herself, Mooky's beautiful tail thumped gently on the floor as she anticipated a ride in the car. She had been on her best behavior lately by not peeing in the house or barking at the cat that lived up the street. She started panting slightly as Vivien walked by, facing the possibility that she would not get to go.

She laid her head on her paws, never taking her eyes off Vivien, and wondered where they might be going and if there would be other dogs there. The suitcase never went to the park and sometimes Mooky was not allowed to go where the suitcase went. If that happened, Vivien would be gone for a while and her friend Lenny would come over to feed her, let her outside or take her for walks. She always loved to see Lenny and his dog Buddy, but she would really prefer to go with Vivien. Mooky desperately wanted to start another adventure.

The phone rang and Vivien stopped what she was doing to talk into it, sounding happy and excited. Mooky's tail thumped on the floor as she heard Vivien say "go." She watched and waited for the back door to open so that she could run out towards the car and claim her spot.

Chapter 2

"Are you sure you can't go, Will? Can't the DC Metropolitan Police do without your services for a few days?" asked Vivien. She had the phone pushed tight against her ear, hoping the answer would change but at the same time knowing that it wouldn't.

"I wish I could, ma'am, but we had that messy homicide in Capitol Heights last week and everybody is pulling double shifts. The chief says maybe Sunday I could get out early, but we won't know until you're already gone. How far away is this place you're going?"

Vivien was sad Will couldn't make it, but at the same time she was also a bit concerned that the arrangements might be awkward, since Lenny was going. She had two men in her life, the macho but sweet police detective Will Evans who she was dating, and her best friend, the fifty-something, bald, gay, and very funny psychotherapist, Dr. Leonard Thomas, whom she always called Lenny. The two men mostly got along just fine, but from time to time she was aware that each was squirming a bit in the other's company.

"It's called Briar Hill and it's about three hours by car. It's really beautiful Will, and they have a hot tub where I was hoping to see you without your trunks." She felt herself blush as she said it, but she didn't care; she wanted to try all of her charms to get Will to set aside his policeman duties and have some fun.

"I'm not sure anybody wants to see that, Viv, but it is a tempting offer. Maybe Lenny will go skinny-dipping in the hot tub with you."

"I'm sure he would, but the end result would not be satisfying for either one of us."

"Roger that. Tell you what, send me the link to the place. If I can get out early, I'll hightail it up there on Sunday, show you what's under my trunks, and we can hang out together on Monday. Deal?"

It was Labor Day weekend, so most of the country was off on Monday, except for people in the service industry and dedicated first responders like Will.

"I accept your terms and intend to hold you to them, Detective."

"Fair enough. You're taking the dog, right?"

"Yes, Mooky is going and so is Buddy. That's part of the reason we picked this place, it's dog-friendly with lots of fields and woods for them to run through."

"She's going to love it. Is she sitting by the door?"

"She's lying in the kitchen so she can see both doors, but pointing towards the back where the car is." Vivien looked down at Mooky who, right on cue, thumped her tail, glanced towards the back door, and began panting. "And I'm pretty sure she knows that something is up."

"Sure she does," said Will. "That's the smartest, human-bone-finding dog in town. If she were a bit younger, I would have her drafted to the Metro PD."

"Well that's not going to happen, she is semi-retired, like me. All right, I gotta go honey, Lenny is not a patient traveler."

"I know. Listen, I love you, be careful, have fun, and hopefully I'll see you on Sunday."

"I sure hope so, Detective. I love you too. I'll call you when we get there and leave a message."

"Perfect," said Will, and the line went silent.

He was, as always, to the point and sometimes abrupt, but he did say the magic words without being prompted. She returned to packing and organizing with one eye on the clock. She had volunteered to drive, and to pick Lenny up. As she sorted through underwear, tops, jeans, and sweaters, her mind drifted back to the big changes her life had been through in the past year.

Her crazy dog had found a human leg bone in Rock Creek Park during one of their regular visits to the not-quite-legal dog park known as Doggie Hill. The bone eventually prompted a search that revealed the earthly remains of Phyllis, one of the dog park regulars nobody really liked. Phyllis had been having a secret affair with Sasha, another one of the dog park regulars, who was involved in Phyllis's death but not formally charged with anything.

As a retired Secret Service agent, Vivien had loved being involved in an active police investigation and was now toying with idea of trying to market herself as a private investigator. The back injury that knocked her out of active duty still flared up sometimes, but she'd lost ten pounds after the 'Phyllis incident,' got a shorter, more contemporary hairstyle, and found the gumption to clean and organize her house into respectable shape.

Her romance with Will seemed to be mostly on course, her friendship with Lenny remained a stabilizing and amusing presence in her life, and her dog had been on her best behavior lately. She had nothing to complain about and few worries. As she double-checked to make sure the coffee pot was off, she had no inkling that she was about set off another adventure that would be sparked by her dog's finely tuned nose.

Chapter 3

"So, Viv, who do you think our fellow travelers will be at this charming country inn you've done such a fine job of locating? I wonder if there will be any hot, single travelers that might, you know, be of like minds with moi." Lenny was wearing sunglasses that looked a bit too large for his face and was watching the scenery on the interstate fly by at 67 miles an hour, the speed Vivien punched into the cruise control. Her plan was to go two miles an hour over the limit, which was not enough to attract any attention from her brothers and sisters in law enforcement. At least that's what a state patrolman had told her once.

"I thought we were going so you and I could have some fun, run the dogs, do some hiking and maybe some antiquing, not turn you loose on a booty call with traveling strangers," said Vivien.

"This trip is hardly a booty call, sweetie, and yes, of course we shall do all those things. I'm just saying, a lot of these B and B places are set up so that you do some mingling, that's all. I enjoy meeting new people, don't you?"

"Sure I guess. Since the place appeals to couples, I guess we might meet somebody. I was really hoping Will could get off, since you and I are now an odd couple sleeping in two separate rooms by ourselves. We could have just shared a bed, you know, and saved some money."

"Well, I do appreciate that Viv, but firstly, if the lunk does show up you two will need the space. Second, I have it on good authority that I snore like a freight train, and third, two people, two dogs, and one bed. I just think it's too much. It's better this way, trust me. Not that I would kick you out of bed, Ms. Szabo." He reached over and lightly pinched her cheek. "You are cute as a button. I hope Officer Will knows what a lucky man he is."

"Detective Will, and yes he does. He said the 'L word' to me on the phone today."

"Lesbian? He asked if you were a lesbian? What did you say? Did you finally fess up?"

"Ha-Ha, very funny. He told me he loved me."

"Oh my, this is getting serious, isn't it? But he's not coming, right?"

"Maybe Sunday. He's working a double homicide and everybody in his division is doing overtime."

"Okay, so probably just me and you and two dogs not named Boo. How much farther is it?"

"Jeez, Lenny, we just started. Another two hours at least. But getting back to that sharing the bed thing. Did you ever...? I mean, were you ever with...? I mean, have you had a...?"

"Have I slept with women, is that what you're asking, Viv? Have we not had this conversation in all the time I've known you?"

"If we have, I can't remember what you said. Wine may have been involved."

"That would not surprise me. The answer is yes. Before I fully embraced my true calling, I dated, courted, and slept with a few women, resulting in a few clumsy interludes that pointed me in the correct direction. Now. How about you? Any experiments along the way?"

Vivien felt herself blush and reached to tune the radio as the station started to break up from the distance now stretching between the travelers and their homes. Both dogs had taken up positions in the back of the minivan. Mooky was lying down on the bench seat. Buddy was curled up on the floor.

Vivien cleared her throat and said, "Well, I probably told you when I was still living in Milwaukee there was another woman on the force who was clearly, well, you know."

"Gay?"

"Right. Gay. Anyway, she made a pass at me, which was kind of shocking. I mean, it wasn't like I'd never been around it or wasn't aware, it just never, you know..."

"Resulted in a direct invitation? So, you what, broke this poor lady's heart and just moved on?"

"I don't think her heart was broken but yes, I did decline the invitation."

"And you never looked back and never considered what might have been?"

"Well, no. I mean, Lenny, she was really, you know…"

"Dykey? She was a big, fat, bull dyke?"

"That's not nice, but yes, she was a big, scary, bull dyke."

They both laughed, feeling a bit naughty, as Vivien found a local radio station. It was the weather portion of a news update, and the radio voice was talking about a tropical storm that was forming off the coast of Cuba, which seemed exotic and very far away. Vivien flipped her hair, adjusted her sunglasses, and stretched her left leg to keep her back from cramping up. "I'm so glad we're doing this," she said. "We're going to have a ball whether Will shows up or not." She smiled at Lenny, who reached over and gave her forearm a playful squeeze.

Chapter 4

Mooky heard the sound of gravel under the car tires and knew this was the time of go. She stood up on the seat, stretched as best as she could in the moving van, wagged her tail slowly and looked out the window to see large trees, green grass and rolling fields. Buddy got up too and looked out his own side of the van, his head bumping against the window, as they got closer. Mooky began to pant as she struggled to keep her balance. New smells were already starting to make their way into the car; woods and black dirt, flowers and new people, and many dogs that had come and gone.

She tried to spin in a circle but the seat and the car's rocking kept knocking her off-balance. She jumped down and squeezed between the two seats where she could smell Vivien and Lenny. She gave Lenny's leg a lick and looked towards the door, telling him she was ready to go out now. She wanted to be outside the van, smelling new things, seeing new things. She felt his hand on her head and his face appeared very close to her.

"Almost there, girl, just hold your horses a few more minutes and we'll let you out." She didn't know what most of those words meant, except for the last one and that was one of best words of all. She definitely wanted to be out. Out in the air, out from the car, out in the time of go. The car stopped, she heard the seat belts pop, and fresh smells began to come into the car as the front doors were opened.

She watched the big door next to her, her ears perked up in complete attention, and then it happened, the door was open and she was out. Out in the green grass beyond the gravel where the car was parked. She was vaguely aware that she had run right by Vivien who was holding her leash and now calling to her, but her voice didn't sound that serious and besides, there were too many smells to explore and she could not wait.

She smelled and peed, smelled and peed, and was now aware that another car was about to open its doors, which meant more people and maybe more dogs. She ran towards the new car wondering who might come out as her tail swooped back and forth.

The door opened and smells of flowers came out but there was no smell of dogs. A man was getting out and looking at her in a strange way that made the hair on her back stand up. He was uncomfortable being near her, which made her instantly defensive. She dropped her head closer to the ground, slowed her pace and got closer, close enough to strike if she had to, and then she began to bark a warning.

A warning that something was wrong with this man and everybody should know about it. She barked louder and faster, putting herself between the man and her friends behind her. Vivien was on the other side of the car and not in immediate danger, but now the man drew back, like he was going to get back in the car or maybe get something out of the car that could hurt Mooky and her friends.

The man was yelling something now, yelling words that Mooky didn't understand, but they sounded mean and threatening. She barked louder and heard herself growling as foam formed on her lips; she moved in a little closer, looking for a soft, unguarded spot on the man where she could grab a hold, pull him away from the car and—

"Hey!" said Vivien. "What is the matter with you? Come over here!" Mooky heard her but she still kept on barking. She heard and felt the leash click onto her collar but even that didn't stop her. She felt Vivien jerk on the leash and now felt herself being pulled away from the man as she half turned towards him, giving a few more warning barks as she was pulled away until she could not see the man anymore. They were saved. She saw Buddy and Lenny and her tail began to wag. The smells were coming back to her, so many smells to explore here in the time of go.

Chapter 5

Vivien was pissed off and a little freaked out that her dog had just about attacked a perfect stranger upon their arrival at the Briar Hill bed and breakfast. She had a firm grasp on the leash as she half-pulled, half-guided Mooky away from the rich guy in the fancy car who hadn't done anything to warrant this kind of totally unacceptable behavior from her dog.

"What the hell has got into you, Mooky? That was very bad. You're going to get us thrown out of here before we even check in. God dammit."

"What was that all about?" said Lenny. He had Buddy on his leash and was standing by the car with a curious look on his face.

"I don't know, she just started barking at that guy who just pulled in. I thought she was going to go after him for a second."

Lenny knelt down and looked Mooky in the face like he was searching for some kind of visible symptom of a malady.

"What's going on, Mook? You didn't like the hoity-toity rich guy?"

"Lenny, that's not nice. He may be a perfectly pleasant man, let's not judge. I need to go over there and apologize. Will you hold her?"

"Certainly madam, I shall stay here with the beasts of the field and await your imminent return."

Vivien smiled to herself at Lenny's funny way of making everything more dramatic, and walked back towards the other guy's car. As she got closer she noted it was a late model, white BMW. The badge on the car's rear read '760i,' which she assumed was the model number. She was keenly aware that the large sedan looked very expensive.

The guy was getting his luggage out of the back seat, which was made of soft brown leather and also looked very expensive. He was wearing tan leather loafers, Gucci maybe, with jeans that looked like they'd been dry-cleaned and pressed.

He was wearing a white, long-sleeved shirt open at the collar, and a tan leather belt. The cuffs of his shirt had been flipped up to reveal a thin-faced watch held to his tanned wrist by a brown leather strap.

As she got closer she could smell his cologne, subtle and pleasing, causing her to smile as she approached.

"Hi there. Listen, I'm terribly sorry about my dog, she's really quite friendly. I'm sorry if she startled you."

The guy was wearing sunglasses as he extricated himself from the back seat, holding a bag in one hand and a sport coat in the other. He was holding the sport coat in an odd way, and as he turned towards her, Vivien could see that it was draped over a pistol in a brown leather holster. She could only see the butt of the grips but she was positive it was a Glock 19. The guy slammed the door and moved closer to her, making no move to further conceal the weapon.

"Oh, so that's your mutt? I'll tell you what, lady, if that dog comes near me again I will blow its fucking head off with no hesitation. Comprendo? I don't know if they have leash laws in wherever the fuck you are from but I'm sure as hell not going to be attacked out here in the boonies by your stupid animal. Stay away from me and keep your dog on a leash."

As he turned away, Vivien realized she had her hand sticking out thinking she would introduce herself once she finished apologizing, but clearly that was not going to happen. He brushed by her leaving a wake of cologne behind as she realized there was something familiar about his tanned, handsome face and the shock of well-coiffed gray hair covering his head. His voice was familiar too; she'd seen him somewhere – maybe on TV.

He walked around the back of the car and Vivien noticed a tall, dark-haired woman standing under the tree waiting for him. She was wearing high, open-toed heels that revealed a fleet of bright red toenails.

She had long, tanned legs and was wearing a short, dark-colored tailored dress that looked too hot and formal for the setting.

She looked fit and well-maintained as she stared into her phone through a pair of oversized sunglasses while jabbing at the keys with long red fingernails. Red lipstick completed the ensemble, and her dark tresses were partially pinned up off her slender neck. She was fashion model pretty but also looked like she was nobody to trifle with.

The guy brushed by her like she wasn't there and said over his shoulder, "Come on Rachel, time to check in with the Clampets. I cannot believe you fucking talked me into this."

Vivien became aware that she was still standing in the driveway with her hand out, waiting to shake with somebody who had just insulted her, threatened to kill her dog, and was now on his way inside the inn. She dropped her hand, cleared her throat and walked back towards her minivan, her head swimming a bit from the verbal and emotional onslaught. She got back to Lenny who was standing in the same location and now asked, "Well, what did he say? Everything patched up?"

"Not exactly. He told me he'd shoot Mooky if she got anywhere near him, and he seems to be carrying a pistol under his jacket."

"So, he's as big a jerk in real life as everybody says he is," said Lenny. "Not that surprising, I guess. But he showed you a gun? Isn't that illegal or something?"

"He didn't really show it to me, I saw it under his jacket. Glock 19, nine millimeter, fifteen rounds in the mag. An amateur gun-nut favorite. Wait a second, you know him?"

"Me and everybody else, didn't you recognize him? It's Michael Samuels, from the news show."

"Oh my god, you're right. I knew he looked familiar. What the hell is he doing here?"

"Same thing as us, except obviously without a dog, and oh my god, did you see his vampire girlfriend? Everybody who's ever dealt with him says he's just a total dick, and I mean he kind of comes across that way on the show."

"That's right, he's the one that kind of harasses his guests."

"Harasses, berates, makes fun of anybody who doesn't share his extreme right-wing opinions."

"He's right?"

"Very right, all the time. Just ask him. Oh look, here come some more of our fellow travelers." Lenny nodded his head towards a late model Mercedes SUV pulling slowly up the long, gravel driveway. "Should we jump into the check-in line so we don't get lost in the shuffle?" He started to move towards the front door of the inn, but Vivien grabbed his arm and said, "No, wait. I don't want to get anywhere near Mr. TV Newsman. We're already off to a bad start."

"Right, I mean what's the hurry? Let's just stand here in the fresh air and perhaps survey the grounds. Looks like there's a barn or something over here." Vivien and Lenny began walking towards the barn as Vivien took in the scenery. They were way out in the sticks, not far from the Blue Ridge Mountains, and the inn was a Victorian-era farmhouse that had been upgraded and gently added on to over the years.

On the way up, they'd driven by signs pointing the way to vineyards hidden somewhere along the country roads. They'd gone over several bridges stretched over meandering creeks and small rivers, including a covered bridge that Vivien wanted to return to and take some pictures.

The scenery was defined by gently rolling green hills and large mature trees bordering fields planted with rows of waist-high corn. The mountains that could be seen hulking in the background were cast in a bluish gray. The inn sat on a clear spot on top of a small hill. The barn they were walking towards was painted red, smelled like horses, and sat down near the bottom of the hill, along a two-wheeled dirt path leading them forward. The dogs jerked and tugged, anxious to get off their leashes.

They stood admiring the view and walked out to edge of the cornfield as Vivien noted the well-kept look of the grounds. She said, "It's really beautiful and peaceful, isn't it?"

Lenny wrapped his arm around her shoulders and said, "You have chosen well, grasshopper. Come on, he should be gone by now."

They headed back towards the parking area as the people in the SUV had just finished getting all their bags out of the vehicle and were letting their dog walk around and sniff. The dog was a beautiful setter, or maybe a spaniel of some sort, Vivien had trouble identifying the sub-breeds, but she was pretty sure it was a Brittany.

The woman holding the leash was a pretty Asian girl, dressed fashionably in suede-colored jeans, a nearly matching jacket, and high-heeled boots. She looked very comfortable holding the dog. The guy she was with closed the rear hatch of the vehicle and came around towards them. He was tall, good looking, with dark hair, also dressed nicely in jeans, Timberland boots, a trendy, checkered shirt, chunky sports watch and his own version of a suede leather jacket. The three of them were quite an attractive group. Mooky pulled at her leash wanting to get a sniff of the setter.

"Oh, she's beautiful," said Vivien and nodded towards the dog. "Is she a spaniel?"

"Yes," said the Asian girl. "Your dog is beautiful as well, nothing like a lab, right? What's her name? Is she friendly?"

"Her name is Mooky and yes, she will friend you to death."

The Asian girl laughed and covered her mouth slightly with her hand. "Okay then Mooky, say hi to Keisha."

The two women moved closer to let the dogs sniff each other as their tails wagged faster. Lenny joined the group and now all three of the dogs were stretching, scratching, and sniffing anxiously, pulling on their leads, eager to run and tear through the fields.

"Looks like everybody is getting along, huh?" said the tall guy as he walked over carrying suitcases in both hands.

Lenny looked him up and down and said, "The human race can take a lesson here, eh old chum? My name is Leonard, that's my friend Vivien over there, and the dogs are Buddy and Mooky. Who are you two wonderfully attractive people?"

Vivien felt herself blush a bit. You never really knew what was going to come out of Lenny's mouth. He was charming, but sometimes his flattery embarrassed her. Luckily, the attractive couple didn't seem to mind, as they both smiled.

"I'm Tom Stoddard, this is my wife Amy, and of course you've already met Keisha."

"Charmed, I'm sure," said Lenny. "First-time visitors here?"

"Yes, we heard good things about it and drove up from DC. Great to get out of the city and see some nature and shit," said Tom.

"Exactly," said Lenny, "nothing like nature and shit. Speaking of which, unless my nose is playing tricks on me I think there are horses in that barn."

"According to the website there are," said Amy. "I can't wait to get back in the saddle."

"Don't you worry about that, baby, I intend to spend a lot of time in the saddle with you over the next few days. I hope you brought your riding crop, HA!" said Tom. Vivien smiled as Lenny's eyebrows shot up toward the top of his bald skull.

Amy smiled a small grin, looked at Tom sideways and slowly shook her head as she said softly, "Such a naughty boy, aren't you?" He sidled up next to her and gave her a quick hug as they all heard the unmistakable country sound of a screen door slamming.

The dogs perked up their ears, and all heads turned towards the front to see Michael Samuels walking towards them with an older man trying to keep up. Rachel the apparent girlfriend also emerged, looking at the nails on one hand and holding a phone up to her ear with the other. She took long, graceful, unhurried strides in heels.

Samuels strode purposely towards them as Tom Stoddard checked his pockets and then turned back towards his car as if he'd forgotten something. He opened the car door and began rooting around as the Samuels party came to a stop next to his white BMW.

"So here's the problem," said Samuels. "You've got this parking area set up right here under this tree. You know who likes trees?" He was talking to the older guy who was wearing jeans, a brown Carhartt jacket, a well-worn checkered shirt, work boots and a John Deere hat. Vivien assumed this was the innkeeper, or a local farmer who had somehow walked into the Michael Samuels shit show.

"Far as I know, just about everybody loves trees, sir. What's the problem?" asked the older man.

"Birds. Birds are the problem. Birds roost in trees, birds poop on car, guest unhappy. See where I'm going with this, Einstein? I can't park here. I want to move my car to a safer location, like maybe that barn over there. Or do we say 'yonder' here? Over yonder. That barn. My car. Inside. Where's the keys to the barn?"

"Oh, I'm sorry sir, the barn isn't for guests' cars. I have horses in there. Really isn't any room to park cars in there."

"No room? Bullshit. Look at it. My car goes in the barn or you agree to pay for damages when these fucking country birds shit all over my car. Dealio?"

Before the old man could react to the latest offering from Samuels, Rachel caught up with the rest of the group and said, in a voice that seemed too calm for the occasion, "Michael, Chuck's on the phone and he's got the overnights. Perhaps you'd like to speak to him?"

Samuels's head snapped towards her and then back to the old man, whose face had taken on a harder look. "I'll deal with you later, pops." He turned to walk towards Rachel but stopped dead in his tracks in front of Amy, who had a firm grip on her dog's lead and was watching the whole scene unfold with a critical eye. Samuels leaned in towards her and said, "Well konnichiwa, gorgeous, what room are you staying in?"

"First of all, I'm Chinese, and secondly, I don't know as I haven't checked in with my husband yet."

Samuels shot a glance at Tom, who was now searching the trunk, and said, "Hmmm. Well, let me know when you get it sorted out, right?"

Samuels took a step towards Rachel and practically grabbed the phone out of her hand as she coolly looked at him with semi-closed eyelids, like she was shielding herself from his negative energy. He then walked off towards the field by himself, jabbering into the mouthpiece about the show's ratings from the night before.

Tom rejoined the group and held up a riding crop. "Found it honey, great news. What did I miss?"

Before Amy could answer him Rachel took two steps closer to the group and said, "Hi everybody, sorry Michael is being so difficult. He's under a lot of pressure. I'm Rachel, by the way, his producer and sometime handler on his days off. Please forgive him if he seems angry but it's what he does. I keep telling him that one day he's going to insult the wrong party and *bang-bang*, he'll be dead, right? Just kidding. See you all around the campfire." She then laughed like she was the only one in on the joke. She gave the group a half wave and started walking back towards the inn.

Samuels continued railing against whoever was on the phone, gesturing wildly while walking farther away from the group towards the cornfield. As Rachel walked past Tom, she noticed the riding crop and said, "Whoa-ho, I want to party with you cowboy – kidding!" and then gave his arm a squeeze before continuing her saunter back towards the inn.

Tom looked at his arm where Rachel had touched him, then at the group, and said, "What the hell just happened? Who was that, and who's the guy on the phone? He looks like that TV news guy."

"Yep," said the old man, "he's that TV news guy all right, and I think his friend is right. He goes on running his mouth like that around here and somebody is liable to take exception to it. Come on, let's get you folks checked in before I say something I shouldn't."

"Total ass-hat," said Amy.

"Why? What did he say to you?" asked Tom.

"Nothing, Tom. He said nothing. Just let it go, okay?" said Amy.

"No. I want to know what he said. I want to know right now."

"I told you, let it go. The last thing we need is another run-in. Apparently he thinks I'm Japanese or something. Grab the bags, I'll take the dog. Come on."

Amy began guiding Tom towards the front door and out of earshot as he lowered his head and continued to pepper her with questions.

Lenny turned towards Vivien, raised an eyebrow and said, "Well. Quite a group, huh?"

Vivien exhaled long and loud while looking down at her dog who was focused like a laser beam on the still ranting and gesticulating Michael Samuels.

"Yep. I guess Mooky was right about that one. Look at her, she really doesn't like him for some reason."

Lenny half-turned towards the front door of the inn, but Vivien grabbed his arm and stopped him.

"Does the other guy look familiar to you?"

"Who? Our version of Bob Newhart, the folksy innkeeper?"

"No the other guy, the young guy. I think he said his name is Tom Stoddard."

Lenny turned his head to look at the attractive couple walking behind the innkeeper as he was talking and pointing towards the shadowy figures of the Blue Ridge Mountains along the distant horizon.

"I don't think so. Kind of funny playing with the riding crop and all, but he doesn't look familiar to me. Why, do you think you know him?"

"There's something about that name that rings a bell," said Vivien. "I just can't put my finger on it. Plus his girlfriend said something odd. Something like, 'we don't need another run-in.' What do you suppose that means?"

"I couldn't fathom a guess. Mysteries abound. Can we move on now so we can unpack and get these animals fed?"

"Sure," said Vivien, "just my overactive imagination at work again. Let's go." They walked towards the inn as Vivien noted the sky had turned to a low ceiling of gray as far as she could see, and the air felt thicker and heavy. They entered a rustic foyer with naturally stained beadboard along the walls, oversized hooks for coats, and a side table and mirror combination that displayed brochures from local wineries and other nearby attractions. A small desk stood in an alcove under the stairs. Tom and Amy were just finishing their check-in, and brushed by them all smiles as they herded Keisha, the spaniel, past.

The happy tails of the dogs wagged as Vivien and Lenny approached the desk and picked up their keys from the innkeeper, whose name was not Bob but actually Wayne, who explained the house rules.

"Obviously we're dog-friendly here but we ask that you leave them in your room during meals. Some people aren't comfortable around them, and anytime we're ever had any trouble it was usually related to food."

"Right," said Lenny. "That would only make sense."

"We do the brunch buffet from 8 am to 11, after that you're on your own. Couple of decent restaurants in town, and there's more if you want to drive into Staunton, which is about an hour north of here. Other than that, enjoy your stay and let me know if I can point you in the right direction to something." He smiled and gave a single nod of his head to signal the presentation was over. Vivien instantly liked him, as he reminded her of her uncle back in Wisconsin, the one who had taught her squirrel hunting when most girls her age were baking cakes in ovens warmed by a light bulb.

She and Lenny picked up their bags and nudged their dogs towards the stairs as the front door opened and a tall, well-groomed man came in and walked towards the front desk. He had salt and pepper hair, a trimmed goatee, and was also dressed upscale casual. New-looking jeans, checkered, fashion forward shirt, nice leather bag that looked like something a doctor might carry on an overnight excursion, and a lightweight wool sport coat.

"Well hello there, traveler," said Lenny as Vivien felt herself blush and wasn't sure why. Somehow, Lenny had a way of making everything sound suggestive, even a casual greeting.

"Am I headed towards the check-in desk?" said the guy. He had a pleasant, deep voice and no discernable accent.

"You certainly are, young man. I would assist you but we're already burdened by these bags and the beasts."

"So I see," said the guy, "and what fine beasts they are. Perhaps I shall see you two later."

"Well, I certainly hope so," said Lenny and he laughed a hearty laugh that echoed off the high Victorian ceilings of the entrance. Vivien shot the new guy a tight smile as she nudged Lenny towards the stairs while trying to keep a grip on her suitcase, briefcase, and the dog who was doing her best to get a smell of the new person. "Hi, and excuse us," said Vivien.

"No problem," said the guy, as they got past and began climbing the slightly tilted stairway to the guest rooms. Vivien heard the screen door slam again and turned her head to see Michael Samuels enter the space.

"Oh Jeez," said Vivien. They got to the top of the stairs, and she checked the numbers on the door as Lenny said, "What?"

"Mr. Wonderful is in the building."

"Who, the hunk we just met?"

"No. The TV guy. It always amazes me how fast you make friends, Lenny."

"I am a social creature," he said and bowed slightly.

She giggled, double-checked her key number and said, "We're down this hall, you're right next door. Want to get settled and meet out front for a dog walk, then figure out dinner?"

"Deal," said Lenny. "Meet you in thirty or so."

Vivien gave him a wave, walked down the hall, and found her room just as a long, rumbling echo of thunder rolled through the valley.

Vivien slid the smooth brass key into the lock and easily twisted the bolt open. The old five-panel door swung wide with a slight creak, and Vivien saw pretty much what she expected: a queen-sized bed made with what looked to be a hand-made quilt; a small, antique desk and chair set in the far corner of the room; lace curtains over the window; hardwood floors, the high-traffic areas covered by rugs, and no TV or phone. "Perfect," she said to herself as Mooky pushed by her and immediately began a thorough sniff test of the room.

Vivien swung her suitcase on top of the bed, laid down for a second to check the firmness of the mattress, and felt herself starting to drift off before realizing she'd left the dog bed in the van. "Be right back," she said to Mooky as she left the room, closing the door behind her and already hearing voices rising from the check-in desk. She recognized Michael Samuels's, saying, "Look, if it's a private businessman whose religious views don't accept it, why should he have to write out 'Congratulations to Sam and Dave' in icing and put two little grooms on the top if it violates what he believes in?"

"And you're saying what? That happens all the time? Religious bakers all over the country are being forced to put little grooms on the top of wedding cakes which, what? Causes them emotional distress because now God won't let them into heaven? I'm sorry but that's just an absurd argument."

Vivien picked her way down the stairs, trying to be quiet about it so she could hear where the argument was going next as she tried to identify the other voice. As she made her way down she could finally see it was the gray-haired guy who had come in last. He had one hand on his hip and was leaning forward into the argument, obviously passionate about his side of the story.

"You call it absurd," said Samuels, "but I'm telling you it's happening every day. This country is going right down the shitter because of freaks like you wanting to be treated just like the normal people."

Vivien was shocked by the name-calling and how fast the argument had escalated in such a short time. She reached the ground floor and glanced over her shoulder to see if the innkeeper was still involved, but saw no sign of him. She purposely tried to avoid eye contact with the combatants, walked away briskly and pulled her keys out. She popped the door of the van open, grabbed the doggie bed, relocked the door and walked slowly back towards the house, really hoping that whatever was going on was now over.

As soon as she reached the screen door she knew it was still going on, because now the voices were louder.

"I'll tell you what," said the gray-haired guy. "You stay the hell out of my bedroom and I'll stay away from your bigoted baker friends." He was jabbing a finger at Michael Samuels, who was standing with his hands on his hips, a sneering half smile on his face.

"I'll tell you what, fruit loops," said Samuels. "If you like that finger I suggest you put it away and go back into the closet where you belong."

"Blow me, asshole," said the guy, as he grabbed his bag off the floor and brushed by Vivien.

"You wish," shouted Samuels behind him and then noticed Vivien standing there watching the exchange. "What's your problem, dog lady?"

"What exactly is *your* problem?" Vivien heard herself say. "You have to be the most angry person I've ever met in my life."

"Yeah, well. That's what sells the popcorn. If you don't like it, you can piss off too."

Vivien did a quick search of her brain for a snappy comeback but found nothing. She had known Michael Samuels for less than an hour and seen him insult and infuriate everyone he had spoken to. She couldn't ever recall interacting with anybody who was so negative and irritating. For a second she considered the possibility that it was all some kind of act. An act that people tuned in to so they could yell at the TV, or maybe cheer on his hatred to feel better about themselves. She broke eye contact and headed up the stairs trying to put the ugly exchange out of her mind, but it lingered like a pizza with too much garlic.

<h1 style="text-align:center">Chapter 6</h1>

Mooky was more than ready to go out. She wanted to go, and she wanted to run. The sun was up and the room was light enough to see but she could tell by the sound that it was raining outside. She'd had a restless night in the new house. There were many new smells and noises to investigate but Vivien was still asleep. She knew because she had just stood up, walked over and looked at her. Mooky had tried to wake Vivien up earlier while it was still dark outside. The rain had started in the dark, slowly at first before gradually getting stronger, faster, and louder.

Something else had happened during the night that Mooky was very curious about. There were strange noises. A car had started, and driven a short distance. Mooky wanted to know who was in the car and if there were any other dogs that might come out to play with her. She'd heard doors opening and other muffled noises that she couldn't identify. She'd barked a warning but Vivien would not start the time of go. She was told to "be quiet, shhhhh, settle down," and, "stop barking." She didn't know what those words meant but she could tell by Vivien's tone that she was not happy

It was hard to smell what was happening from outside because the window was closed, but she had caught a whiff of another animal through tiny cracks in the window frame. Maybe not a dog or a cat but something that lived outside in the grass. She'd smelled the same thing near the big building that they'd walked by earlier. She wanted to go back to that building, and tried to see it from the window. Her breath fogged up the glass, making it hard to see anything.

She'd barked during the night when she'd heard thunder and a popping noise, and tried to get Vivien to let her go out to see what was making the noise. She'd tried to warn everybody in the new house that something was happening in the other building but nobody woke up to let her out into the time of go. Now was the time of go and Vivien must get up.

To make sure that Vivien would not wake up and go without her, Mooky got a running start and jumped onto the bed. She was not allowed on the bed at home without permission, and sometimes she didn't like to sleep on it anyway. It was too soft, too warm, and she could not feel the house moving underneath her, which made it hard to know when to bark a warning.

Now she was on the bed, which was warm and soft. She turned in two circles to tuck her beautiful tail around her and keep her legs under her to feel for any vibrations the house made, but then Vivien opened her eyes and said, "Hey! What are you doing up here? You know you're not allowed on the bed." Mooky dropped her ears and thumped her tail against the soft bed, now very happy that Vivien was awake.

Soon it would be time to eat and see the other dogs. But first was the time of go. As Vivien rolled around in the bed, Mooky looked towards the window, telling Vivien that something was going on out there. She whimpered a bit and started to pant. She thumped her tail on the bed, anxious to be outside. She crawled on her belly towards Vivien's face and laid her paw on Vivien to let her know that this was the time of go. Vivien looked at her, her face half-hidden under the covers, and said, "Seriously? You know we're on vacation, right? We're allowed to sleep-in here." Mooky didn't know what those words meant so she perked her ears and looked at Vivien, waiting for the right word. She glanced outside again, showing Vivien where she wanted to go.

"Do you really have to go?"

And this was the best word of them all. She jumped up on all fours and barked loudly, now very excited that it was finally time. She barked again and jumped a bit on the bed, feeling it bounce underneath her.

She spun in a circle and barked some more till Vivien said, "Stop, stop, okay, okay we'll go." Vivien guided her off the bed, said "Shhh," and began putting on her clothes, which meant this was definitely the time of go.

Mooky tried to control herself but it was hard, there was much to see and smell in this place. She pressed her nose against the door and swooped her tail, waiting for the door to open. She could hear Vivien putting on her shoes, which was a good sign, and her tail wagged a bit faster. She waited for what seemed like forever and then sensed Vivien's knee next to her. "Okay, back up. Come on Mooky, I can't get the door open with you standing in front of it." Mooky felt herself being pushed back; she smelled her leash but didn't feel it click into place.

The door opened and she could smell food and coffee from downstairs. She walked through the door, down the hall, and could smell Buddy. "Wait, Mooky." She felt her collar tighten and she was stopped in front of Buddy's door. Vivien knocked softly on the door and it opened and she could see Lenny, and Buddy behind him.

"Morning. Ms. Thing here wants to go walkies. Are you guys up yet?"

"Indeed we are ma'am. Give us a moment, won't you? In fact how about if we meet you downstairs?"

"Are you alone in there, Lenny?"

"Nobody here but us chickens, be right down."

Mooky didn't know what those words meant but they were walking down the steps and the smells from the kitchen were growing stronger. She could hear the sounds of food preparation coming from somewhere in the back of the house and she wondered if her breakfast was back there. She wanted to eat but mostly she wanted to go out. There were unusual smells coming from outside and she knew something had happened out there last night, and she desperately wanted to be out there as fast as possible.

Vivien was looking at something on the table, so Mooky pointed her nose towards the door, watching to see who might be coming in or going out, while at the same time showing Vivien where she wanted to go.

Lenny and Buddy finally appeared and now the door was opening, and Mooky was out. Out and running through the time of go. She extended her claws into the dirt as the smells hitting her nose pulled her away, away, away from the house. She didn't have to move her head to find the scent because there was no mistaking where it was coming from: the big building they had walked around yesterday.

She was aware that it was cooler than yesterday, and it was raining but it hadn't gotten through her thick coat of soft, black-as-coal fur. She could hear Vivien behind her, calling her, telling her to stop, but it was too late. She would not stop. She found the corner of the barn and sniffed. Someone had been there. She peed quickly on the spot to mark it, lowered her head to the ground and approached the big door, which was standing wide open. She smelled a car and saw it inside the barn, but its smells were not that strong.

The strongest smell in the barn was an animal, and now Mooky could see the animal. It was huge. Bigger than any animal she had ever seen. Her tail wagged slowly and her mouth opened as she began to pant. It moved its head and snorted, which caused her to perk up her ears. Her tail stood out straight and she barked a soft "Woof."

There were many strong smells in the building and she hardly knew where to start as she approached the box the animal was in. She could smell the man she had barked a warning about yesterday, but she couldn't see him. The smell was faint but she knew it was him as it mixed with the other smells in the building. She continued to sniff around the building, watching the large animal out of the corner of her eye as she became aware that Vivien was calling her, and now Mooky could smell her too.

"What has got into you Mooky? You're not allowed to be in here, what is... Oh my god," said Vivien.

Mooky didn't know what most of those words meant but she knew from Vivien's tone of voice that something was very wrong.

Chapter 7

Vivien couldn't fathom what she was looking at. Mooky was standing in the middle of the barn, panting and looking guilty, as she stood right in front of Michael Samuels's beautiful white car, which looked like it had been valet parked right in the center of the barn. To her left stood a horse – a huge black horse. Maybe the biggest horse she had ever seen in her life, standing in a stall.

The front door of the barn was standing wide open and the only source of light in the space was coming from the gray skies currently hanging over the country inn. Apparently it had started raining sometime during the night and it was still coming down in a slow but steady downpour.

Vivien wiped some of the rain from her forehead, took a quick look around for a towel, found nothing and moved cautiously towards the horse. She hadn't had coffee yet; her mind felt sluggish like she was thinking through a filter of mud. She was squinting into the back of the stall, seeing what appeared to be Michael Samuels half-naked and hunched over, as if he'd gotten drunk while standing behind the horse, dropped his pants, and then slid down the wall waiting for sobriety to return.

She could make out his bare, pale legs, the knees bent up near his chin. By squinting and moving closer, Vivien determined that the one eye she could see appeared to be open. She instinctively reached for her cell phone and realized she'd left it in the room, not thinking she would need it for a quick walk with Mooky.

A moving shadow caught her eye and Lenny was next to her, with Buddy now joining Mooky sniffing and peeing in various corners of the barn.

"Where did all this rain come from?" said Lenny, and then, "Isn't this Mr. Arrogant's car?"

"It sure is, and I think that's Mr. Arrogant back there in the stall."

"What? Where? Oh my god. It is him." Lenny approached the horse, and soothingly said, "Okay big fella, easy now, okay, we just want to get a look at the moron in your stall." Lenny slowly reached a hand up as the horse snorted and stomped a foot. Lenny held his position and said, "I know, I know, buddy, come on now," as he reached up and stroked the horse's nose.

Vivien was a bit surprised by this latest development and said, "You seem very comfortable there, Doctor. I didn't know you knew anything about horses."

"Well, my beloved sister is an equestrian, don't you know, so I speak a little horsey. While I have his — and I think he is a he — attention, do you want to see if you can figure out what's going on back there?"

"Sure," said Vivien as she walked to the edge of the stall and looked in. Lenny was still stroking the horse's nose as Vivien confirmed she was looking at the seemingly lifeless remains of newsman Michael Samuels.

"What do you see?" said Lenny.

"Umm. I think he may be dead, or...umm, very unconscious. It's hard to tell and I'm a little nervous about walking in there. Isn't there some kind of rule about walking behind a horse?"

"You would be risking the proverbial 'kick in the head,' which is a good thing to avoid," said Lenny. "Since neither you nor I are well acquainted with this animal, we should try to get a bridle on him and lead him out, or see if we can find the innkeeper and get him to help us."

"I like that plan. Got your phone on you?" said Vivien.

"Left it in the room, but when I checked it this morning I was having a hard time getting a signal, and I think I saw Wayne leaving this morning in his truck."

"Really? No signal at all?"

"We are out in the sticks, girlfriend. Ain't nobody to call for help out here." Lenny had slipped into his black girl voice and waggled his finger, which made Vivien smile for a second until the gravity of the situation snapped her back to reality.

"Well, we have to do something, he may still be alive. Hello? Mr. Samuels? Hello? Oh jeez, Lenny, I think he's dead. What did you say you needed? A bridle? Is that the thing you put over their nose?"

Lenny removed his hand from the horse's nose, moved away from the stall in a smooth, deliberate manner, like he was going for a stroll, and walked towards one wall of the barn which was decorated with hanging bits of horse tack that Vivien did not recognize.

"Ah, here we go," he said as he pulled some kind of brown leather harness off the wall and headed back towards Vivien.

"Okay buddy, let's me and you take a little mosey out to the pasture, what do you say, pal?"

Vivien checked on the whereabouts of the dogs. They were both still sniffing the barn as she started to head back towards the inn to make sure Wayne wasn't somewhere on the estate.

Unfortunately her body was not listening to her brain, as she could not will herself away from the possible crime scene. Instead she watched in amazement as Lenny flipped leather straps around, slowly opened the gate to the stall, confidently walked in and then deftly slid the bridle over the horse's head. He snorted and stamped a few more times as Lenny kept up his steady stream of calming patter. When the horse had settled, he stood with the reins in his hand and looked at Vivien.

"Where shall we go?" he said.

"Can you just take him outside for a second so I can see what's going on back here?"

Lenny nodded, and as Vivien watched he and the horse walked out of the barn. She heard the horse snort a few more times as she walked towards the back of the stall, wishing she had a flashlight, a phone and some back-up.

She walked carefully, trying to avoid disturbing anything, and got close enough to put a finger on Samuel's neck where a pulse should have been, but she felt nothing.

"Holy shit," she said to herself. "Maybe he finally pissed off the wrong person."

She retraced her steps and came outside to find Lenny walking the horse towards a corral she hadn't noticed before.

She broke into a trot, noticed the dogs were following her, and called over her shoulder to Lenny, "I'm going for my phone, and I'll put the dogs back inside. Can you join me back in the barn when I come back? I could use an extra set of eyes."

Lenny put his hand over his heart and said, "At your service madam. I shall put the beast in yonder corral and join you shortly."

Vivien gave him a thumbs-up, called to the dogs to keep them interested, and ran faster towards the inn, wondering if it was now raining harder. She got the dogs inside, ignored the leashes for the moment and ran them upstairs. She found her phone, which had a flashlight app on it and a decent camera. She went to her larger shoulder bag, opened it up and looked at the locked gun case inside. She ran her finger over the textured surface of the case and repeated the digital combination to herself knowing that her Sig Saur 9mm was resting inside with a full magazine of ammunition.

In less than five seconds she could have the case open, the mag in place and a round in the chamber, but she closed the bag and slid it back behind the chair. She didn't need to be armed at this point. Michael Samuels had been rendered harmless. She slid the phone into the front pocket of her jeans and took the staircase quickly back down to the ground floor. She briefly noted the smell of coffee and headed back to the kitchen, which was through a swinging door, and poked her head inside looking for the innkeeper. Instead she saw a small blonde-haired girl working on arranging blueberry muffins onto a serving platter.

"Oh, hi. I was looking for Wayne, is he around by any chance? I'm afraid there's been some kind of an accident out in the barn."

The girl looked like she was trying to figure out what Vivien was saying.

Svetlana looked Vivien in the eye and said, "Accidents will happen, new lady. Wayne has really gone to town on this day. Big wind coming, maybe batten down." Vivien picked up on an accent from somewhere in Europe.

"What?" said Vivien. "Gone to town, where? When is he coming back?"

Svetlana didn't look up, instead concentrating on the muffins, which looked delicious.

"You must excuse me please," said Svetlana. "There is much breakfast for now."

Vivien assumed the girl was from another country, as some broken sentences in Croatian that she'd learned in childhood appeared in her head and then quickly vanished. She was a pleasant looking young lady with a round pretty face, short blonde hair, and the build of a gymnast. "Probably strong as a wire," thought Vivien as she ducked out of the kitchen, came through the front door quickly and felt herself running back towards the barn.

Lenny was just finishing tying the horse to a rail on the corral, then joined her at the front door of the barn. The rain was falling steadily but the horse didn't seem to mind.

"So Wayne is apparently in town," said Vivien.

"Yep. I thought so," said Lenny.

They were both squinting at each other as the rain pelted their faces and the wind began pulling on their clothes. Lenny was quickly becoming soaked, as Vivien remembered the phone in her pocket.

"Come on, let's get out of this rain."

They went back inside the barn and Vivien immediately pulled her phone out and punched 9-1-1 into the keypad, but she was stopped by an annoying warning tone that told her she had no service.

"Seriously?" she said to the useless device. "I just bought this phone. Are we that far from civilization?"

"Yelp said cell service was spotty out here," said Lenny as he wiped rain from his forehead with the back of his hand and reached into his pocket with his other to produce a hanky which he handed to Vivien. "Here," he said. "It's clean."

Vivien took the hanky, thanked Lenny, and found the flashlight app on her phone. She turned it on and shined it towards the back of the stall.

Lenny stepped up beside her, looked towards where she was pointing, and said, "The douche bag appears to be missing his trousers."

"He does, doesn't he? Are you okay with this? I mean, taking a closer look? The last time we went through this with the bones, you seemed a bit squeamish."

"Bones creep me out. I will admit that. As a child, at Halloween? Honey, those kids in the skeleton costumes inspired nightmares. But dead dumbasses? Not an issue. Let's proceed, shall we?"

Vivien moved her hand to scan the light around the stall, and said, "I just don't want to contaminate the crime scene by trampling over a clue."

"Crime scene? How do you know he wasn't kicked to death by a horse that knows a horse's ass when he sees one? I vote for accidental death via old Equus out there in the corral. Besides, we are literally in the middle of Bumfuck, I do not see the local authorities sending in the CSI team to investigate this. Do you?"

"That's not the point. If there has been foul play we can't be in there disturbing the evidence."

"I understand," said Lenny. "Since you are the expert here, why don't we take a look using the proper protocol that you learned back in Po-Po school."

"Okay, good deal. Follow my lead, and keep your eyes open for clues," said Vivien.

Vivien held the light over her head and then remembered that her camera would also shoot video. She found the button, turned it on, held the phone over her head and began narrating their preliminary investigation.

"This is Vivien Szabo, former U.S. Secret Service agent, former City of Milwaukee Police Officer, and Dr. Leonard Thomas, on Saturday the first of September inside a barn located at the Briar Hill Bed and Breakfast in Spotsylvania County in Virginia." Vivien began slowly moving towards the back of the stall, watching the ground below her and moving the light in semi-circles in front of her.

"My dog Mooky ran into this barn at approximately 8:15 this morning and began barking. Upon arrival I noticed what appeared to be the body of one of the guests here, a Michael Samuels."

Vivien bent down and shined the light directly onto Samuels and noticed for the first time what appeared to be a gunshot wound on the right side of his head.

"Cause of death could be a gunshot."
Lenny interrupted her by saying, "Excuse me, Ms. Marple, but you might want to have a look at the other side." He was pointing at something.

Vivien moved carefully in front of the body, once again minding where she was stepping and looking for footprints. She looked to where Lenny was pointing and noticed the clear impression of a hoofprint on the left side of Samuels's forehead. There was also a large exit wound towards the back of the skull, and a leather belt looped loosely around his neck.

"The body has also suffered a head wound that appears to have been inflicted by the horse that was found in the same stall as the body. I'm also seeing a brown leather belt looped around the victim's neck. The victim's pants and underwear are down around his ankles for reasons unknown at this time."

"Is he dead?" said a voice that came from behind them.

Vivien's heart jumped as she felt her instincts pull her hand to where her gun would be, but her brain stopped her. She spun around and aimed her phone at the voice, which belonged to Amy, the pretty Asian girl they'd met yesterday in the parking lot.

"What are you doing in here?" said Vivien in a voice that sounded more authoritative than friendly.

"Is the asshole dead?" asked Amy.

"Quite dead I'm afraid," said Vivien. "I would ask you not to come any further, this could be an active crime scene."

Amy raised her hand and said, "Hey, no worries, I don't need to intrude on your cops and robbers stuff, but I am a doctor in case you need an official reading."

Vivien dropped the phone to hip level and said, "What kind of doctor? Medical?"

"ER," said Amy, "and from here I'd say your assumption is correct: he appears to be deceased."

Vivien scanned the floor of the barn between them and Amy one more time for any footprints they could be walking over, saw nothing, and said, "Well if you are a doctor and can take a quick look I wouldn't mind hearing your thoughts."

Amy didn't wait for a second invitation and stepped confidently towards the body. "Did you call 911?" she asked.

"Tried to, but neither one of us has a signal out here," said Vivien.

"I'm sure the hurricane isn't helping," said Amy. "Shine your light back here, and let's take a look."

"Hurricane?" said Lenny. "Is that what's happening?"

"They're calling it Betty," said Amy. "It's coming right up the coast faster than anybody thought, pushing another minor storm in front of it and soaking everything along the way."

She bent down, pulled Vivien's phone hand closer to the body, put two fingers on Samuels's neck and looked closely at the belt. "Probably his own belt. Shot in the head, kicked by the horse, somehow lost his pants, and half covered in manure. Went out in a blaze of glory huh, dickhead? And what a small dick it is. Figures."

Vivien tried not to look between Samuels's legs but did note that a large pile of horse crap covered his feet. "Umm, any theories on cause or time of death?"

"Take your pick," said Amy as she stood up. "You need a coroner, an M.E., maybe an autopsy to figure out actual cause. Shot and then strangled? Strangled, then shot? Who knows. Any sign of the gun?"

"No," said Vivien. "How about time?"

Amy shrugged. "Had to be last night, right? We all saw him yesterday when he was alive and pissing everybody off. Looks like he got his just desserts."

"That's for the law to decide, don't you think?" said Vivien.

"Whatever you say, lady. I'm satisfied that karma has been served. Are you a cop by any chance?"

"Retired," said Vivien as she looked at Amy with narrowing eyes. "When was the last time you saw our friend here?"

"Pretty sure you were there, weren't you? We went into town for dinner last night but didn't run into him. I'm going to go back to my room and get my phone to see if I can get a signal. Even a jerk like him deserves to have his remains looked after, and I don't think the horse should be left out in the rain. See ya'll back at the ranch. God, what a mess."

She brushed her hands together like she was trying to remove some dust from her fingers, turned and walked quickly out of the barn without another word.

Vivien looked at Lenny and said, "Well. That was an interesting exchange. What do you think?"

"I'd call her suspect number one," said Lenny.

Chapter 8

Vivien decided there had to be a landline in the house, especially with the spotty cell service and the fact that Wayne was running a business. She and Lenny draped a horse blanket over the body of Michael Samuels and began walking back to the house, her mind ticking through possible murder scenarios and suspects. Besides Amy the doctor there was Amy's handsome husband Tom, Wayne the innkeeper who was currently absent, Rachel, the new guy who checked in late by himself, Svetlana the muffin maker, and, of course, Lenny – who was probably not the assailant.

The rain continued a relentless pelting and Vivien wondered how she could have missed the news reports about an approaching hurricane. The radio said something about a tropical storm in Cuba that was expected to turn west. Maybe she was just too preoccupied getting ready for the trip, but the weather had definitely arrived and was wreaking havoc on their plans. "Do you think our getaway weekend is already ruined, Lenny? We're off to a horrible start, and I can't believe a hurricane somehow managed to sneak up on us."

"Oh I was aware of it, but they were saying they expected it to turn west towards the gulf. What we're seeing here isn't even the hurricane yet. This is the storm that was supposed to stay down south for the weekend, but I do take your point, dog walking and antiquing seems to be taking a back seat to crime solving and clue gathering."

They reached the front porch and Vivien turned to face him, watching the rain drip off his eyebrows. "Maybe this is a sign," she said. "Maybe we should just get back in the van and get out of here right now. Leave this to the local cops, head back home, maybe buy some wine and ride the storm out from the safety of our own comfy living rooms."

Lenny looked at her with a deadpan face as skepticism began to slowly wash across it. "Really Viv? That's what you want to do? Dead body in the barn, no communication with the outside world, major storms heading this way and you want to go home and drink wine. Is that right? That's what you really want to do?"

The question hung in the air as the rain pounded the earth and a gust of wind blew a sheet of water at them. Vivien wiped her forehead, thought about Michael Samuels, dead by a variety of causes, his car in the barn, the innkeeper's possible motives, the odd girl in the kitchen, the mysterious lone traveler, Samuels's traveling companion, the pretty Asian doctor, and the handsome husband with a temper.

"No. It's not what I want to do," said Vivien. "Not by a long shot. Let's find that phone."

"Good," said Lenny as he followed her into the building.

The smells of breakfast greeted their return. Bacon, eggs, fried potatoes, sausage, and toast were laid out on a sideboard in the dining room along with a bowl of fruit salad, a pot of coffee, and a selection of teas. Svetlana was moving like a cat, freshening the bowls and tidying up. Rachel, the self-identified handler of the dead man, was sitting at the table wearing a black hoody made from a silky fabric with a yet untouched cup of black coffee, a bagel, and a single cube of pineapple in front of her. She was staring into her phone.

Lenny said, "I'll go up to the rooms and check on the dogs if you want to look for the phone." Vivien gave him a wave indicating that she approved the plan and turned her attention to Rachel. "Are you able to get a signal?" asked Vivien, "because neither one of us are getting any bars."

"Excuse me? Oh, no, I have nothing but yesterday's news," Rachel replied. "Must be the rain or something because it was working fine yesterday."

"Or the wind knocked down the cell tower," said Vivien. "When was the last time you saw your boss?"

"Um, last night. Why, are you taking a poll?" she replied without looking up, adding, "and 'boss' is kind of a stretch."

Vivien felt the back of her neck heat up at the smart aleck response. "So, I guess you haven't seen him yet this morning?"

Rachel looked up, her face devoid of makeup. She looked older and plainer but still attractive, Vivien thought.

"Haven't you heard? Michael Samuels is a media genius who comes and goes as he pleases. He does not report to me, or anybody else on this planet that I know of – not that this is any of your business."

Vivien crossed her arms in front of her and cleared her throat. "Well, Rachel, the media genius, or what's left of him, is dead out in the horse barn. Looks like somebody shot him in the head then strangled him, or vice versa, so I'll ask you again, when was the last time you saw him?"

Rachel swallowed, took a sip of coffee, and said "What? What did you say about the barn?"

Vivien observed little change in the woman's demeanor, which was a bit surprising considering what she'd just told her. She took a step closer to her and laid a hand on Rachel's upper arm, feeling a strong, confident limb underneath the stylish yet casual garment.

"Something terrible has happened to Michael. We found his body out in the barn and it looks like somebody murdered him. We need to call the police and they're going to need to know where everybody was last night. I'm assuming there's got to be a landline here, and as soon as we find it we're calling 911."

"The phone is by the front desk," said Rachel, now gazing off into the distance. "But I'm not sure we should tell anybody just yet. I'd kind of like to confirm what you're saying, first. Does that make sense?"

"What are you talking about?" said Vivien. "What do you mean, 'confirm'? He's out in the barn. Amy 'confirmed' that he's passed. We need backup as soon as possible."

Rachel was still staring off into space and talked like she wasn't really addressing Vivien. "He's in contract negotiations with the network. We just FedExed the documents. This doesn't make any sense. How can he be dead in a fucking barn? Who are you again?"

Vivien brought her face closer to Rachel's. "My name is Vivien Szabo. I'm a retired Secret Service agent. Your boss, or whatever he is, or was, is in the barn with a hole in his head and his pants pulled down around his ankles. He's dead, and half naked. Does that make sense?"

Rachel looked at her with an expression that Vivien could not read. "Okay, Vivien Szabo, retired Secret Service agent, but if we're calling the police to report the death of Michael Samuels, it will only be a matter of time before the press finds out. I would like to see the body, since I am your only link to his next of kin. That's the legal thing to do here, isn't it? Show me the body and I'll let you call whoever you want. Which way is the barn?"

"No," said Vivien. "I don't need anybody's permission to call the police and I can't allow you to do that. The barn is an active crime scene. Nobody goes in or out without me," said Vivien.

"I want to see the body, right now, immediately." Rachel stood up and dropped the phone into her pocket, just as Wayne the innkeeper came through the front door, shaking off rain and stamping his feet. Vivien considered going upstairs for her gun as the situation seemed to be escalating but instead waited for Wayne to appear in the dining room, which he did, as Lenny also came down the stairs.

Vivien looked at Wayne and watched his face carefully as she said, "Wayne, we need to use your phone. Something happened in the barn last night and Michael Samuels is dead."

"What? The obnoxious news guy? Dead in the barn? My barn?"

"We need to use the phone, sir, and I need everybody to stay out of the barn until the police arrive," said Vivien.

Rachel came around the table and now stood between Vivien and Wayne.

"Actually Wayne, this is the story according to Ms. Szabo. No one else has corroborated. Since I am traveling with the allegedly deceased person, I intend to see for myself."

Lenny said, "Actually I can corroborate, I can assure you that he is quite dead. I have seen the barn, as has our friend Amy, who happens to be a doctor. Mr. Samuels has stomped his way off this mortal coil and the proper authorities must be notified as soon as possible."

Wayne pointed at the front desk and said, "The phone is back there, but I'll be surprised if it works. This weather has the whole county screwed up. Young lady, if what they are saying is true I would ask you to do as they say and stay put till we get this sorted out. Now, I have a question, why is my horse out in the corral?"

"I walked him out there because the deceased was found in the back of his stall," said Lenny.

Wayne's mouth shifted like he was trying to solve a riddle. "This is all quite peculiar. Go ahead and try the phone, then I'd like to have a look at whatever is going on in my barn. Are you some kind of a cop, ma'am? Seems like you've done this before," he said while looking at Vivien.

"Secret Service, retired, and the Milwaukee PD," said Vivien as she grimaced at being called "ma'am" and moved towards the phone. She picked it up and was relieved to hear a dial tone. She punched 911 into the keypad and immediately got a busy signal.

"What the hell?" she said to the room. "Nine-one-one is busy."

"Don't surprise me, this weather really has things fouled up," said Wayne. "Come on, let's see the barn."

"I'm going too," said Rachel, "whether you all like it or not."

Vivien couldn't think of a reasonable way to stop everybody from heading back to the barn to view the carnage and she was now questioning how much longer she wanted try to keep things under control. This was Wayne's house not hers.

At the same time she was already making plans in her head for how to keep the amateurs from tampering with the crime scene. The rain was still coming down like it would never stop as the foursome made their way back out to the barn, hands shoved into pockets and shoulders hunched against the weather.

They ducked inside the big door, walked back to the stall and saw… nothing. "Holy shit," said Vivien as she looked at Lenny, who stood, mouth agape, staring at the empty horse stall.

"So this is where you saw him?" asked Wayne. "In the back of this stall, and the horse was in there too?"

"Yes," said Vivien, her brow furrowing with concentration. "I saw him, Lenny saw him, and Amy saw him. We all saw him. Somebody has moved the body."

"Or maybe he's not really dead. Maybe you're making this all up for reasons known only to yourselves," said Rachel. "I'm going to say this again. Announcing the death of Michaels Samuels at this time, without what I believe they call corpus delicti, would be, at best, irresponsible. I've known Michael for many years and I would not be surprised if he's pulled some elaborate prank on you all and is, in fact, right now in the hayloft above us laughing himself silly. Michael Samuels may be a lot of things, but dead in a horse stall is probably not one of them. I implore you to make no announcements until such time as we are positive about what's happening." She turned on her heel, flipped up the hood on her sweatshirt and left the barn.

"I see he managed to get his car in here, protection from the birds or whatever it was," said Wayne.

Vivien moved towards the car, wrapping the hanky Lenny had given her around the door handle and giving it a pull. The door opened as a whiff of leather upholstery, semi-new car smell and cologne momentarily escaped. Vivien checked the ignition but the keys were missing. She closed the door and said, "Maybe the keys are on the body. Maybe the killer has them."

"Ya'll are sure you saw what you think you saw, right?" said Wayne.

"Quite sure, sir," said Lenny. "Dead guy back there, horse right there, car right there. But Rachel's right about one thing, we have definitely lost our corpse. Quite odd. Somebody strong enough to lift the body comes in during the short time we were inside, and moves the body, to where? And for what purpose?"

Vivien looked overhead and spied the hayloft Rachel mentioned, complete with an ancient-looking pulley but no ladder up to it. "Well if we don't have a body, it's much harder to prove foul play, even though we have three witnesses. How long were we inside, five minutes? It's almost like somebody was watching us, waiting for us to leave."

"Either that or they were still in the barn while we were here and waited for us to leave," said Lenny. "Most curious indeed."

Vivien scanned the interior of the barn. She breathed in, trying to detect the smell of anything unusual, but it just smelled like the inside of a cold, damp barn.

She walked to the back of the structure, looking up into the rafters and down onto the dirt floor. Wayne also looked around, like he was taking a quick inventory, and said, "Well. Now what? Can we get the horse back in the barn? Should we move the car? What's the next step?"

Vivien completed her quick inspection and walked back towards the two men. "I don't see any problem with bringing the horse back in, but can we put him in a different stall? There could be, should be, DNA traces of blood and who knows what else in there. Obviously we can't move the car without the keys and I'm sure the cops will want to dust it for prints."

"Yep, I'll put Zeus in the stall next door. He won't know the difference," said Wayne. "In the meantime why don't ya'll try the phone again – it may be working by now." Wayne turned his back on them and walked out into the rain. Vivien turned to Lenny and said, "We did see what we thought we saw, right? This is not a weird dream is it?"

"Not unless we're both having the exact same dream at the exact same time," said Lenny, "which is scientifically impossible. No, we both saw what we saw and the plot is thickening by the minute. That was quite odd that Rachel didn't seem to believe what we were telling her. We have no motivation to lie to her. I swear, I've always heard show business people were a weird bunch."

Vivien scrunched her face into a thinking pose and said, "She is an odd duck, all right. I guess she has a point about not announcing the death, but we don't have any control over the press, nobody does. We still need the police here since we have strong evidence of foul play. Come on, let's try the phone again."

They hunched up against the rain and walked back to the main building as Vivien's mind lasered in on the facts and then shot off on tangents about what she didn't know. No doubt Amy had already told her husband, Tom, who she also wanted to question. Talking to Svetlana would be somewhat problematic due to the language barrier, and there was also the as yet unnamed single traveler.

They walked in through the front door, after shaking off their jackets on the porch. Vivien made a beeline for the phone as Lenny peeled off towards the dining room. She tired 911 again but was met with the same busy signal. She cursed to herself but then noticed a sticker on the wall near the phone with the local numbers for the police and fire department. Just for the heck of it, she dialed the local number and got a ring. She counted six rings and then heard,

"County Sheriff's Office."

"Oh thank God," said Vivien. "My name is Vivien Szabo and I need to report a death at the Brier Hill Bed and Breakfast. One of the guests was apparently killed in the barn last night."

"Hang on a sec," said the female voice, which was quickly replaced by an older male voice with a trace of an accent Vivien could only identify as 'country.'

"This is Sheriff Olsen, how can I help you?"

Vivien repeated herself and the sheriff said, "Okay, can you give me the name of the deceased?"

"Yes, Sheriff, it's Michael Samuels who does the news show on TV. Apparently he's kind of a celebrity. His producer is staying here too and she doesn't want the press involved but obviously we still need some help out here. We found him this morning, shot and strangled in the barn."

There was a long pause, then the sheriff said, "Shot and strangled. Now there's something you don't see every day. Okay, we sort of have our hands full with this storm, half the roads are out due to flash floods and somebody thinks they saw a rabid bear on the other side of the county, but I'll get out there as quick as possible. In the meantime, I need everybody who's checked in to stay put, and please don't move the body."

Vivien put her hand on her hip, leaned on the counter and said, "Well that's one of the weird parts, Sheriff. We saw the body earlier but when we came back it was gone."

The pause was even longer this time. Vivien imagined the sheriff making a face of disbelief, or perhaps outright doubt.

"What do you mean, gone? Gone, as in it's not in the barn anymore?"

"Right. The body has gone missing."

"Okay, well then I don't have to worry about ya'll moving it. You sure the dead guy was really dead?"

"Quite sure, Sheriff. One of the guests is a doctor and she checked him out. No pulse, gunshot wound to the head, and a belt still around his neck."

"That certainly is odd," said the sheriff. "Tell you what, you tell Wayne I'll get out there as soon as possible..."

Vivien could hear the woman's voice in the background saying something about a bear,   and she could tell the sheriff was distracted.

"Yep. Okay. I have to hang up now ma'am. I'll be there as soon as I can."

Then the line went dead.

As she hung up the phone, Vivien heard somebody coming down the stairs and she stepped out into the room to see Tom, Amy's husband, dressed in jeans and a different checkered shirt. He fluffed his hair, walked by her and began circling the breakfast table. "So my wife tells me the news guy is dead in the barn."

"That's right, Tom. Can you tell me where you were last night?"

Tom picked up a plate, grinned, and said, "Where do you think, ma'am? We're in a bed and breakfast in the middle of nowhere. I was in the parlor having tea and crumpets."

Vivien couldn't help but smile back. He was naturally funny, exuding a kind of boyish charm that was irresistible. No wonder Amy married him.

"That's very funny, Tom, but we may have a murderer amongst us and I'm trying to keep everybody safe, so would you mind giving me a clue about your whereabouts?"

Tom took a step towards her and leaned in close enough for Vivien to smell his scent, a mix of shaving cream and deodorant that was not unpleasant. "I was upstairs, in my room, having some quality time with my wife, if you know what I mean?"

Vivien felt herself blush and couldn't stifle a giggle. "I think I do, sir. I'm assuming Amy will corroborate that. Can I ask if you saw Mr. Samuels anytime during the, um, proceedings?"

"Not unless he was hiding in the closet. But seriously, what the hell is going on? Has somebody called the cops or an ambulance or something?"

"The sheriff is coming out as soon as he finishes dealing with a rabid bear situation."

"Rabid bear situation? Wow, we really are out in the boonies. I must say, if somebody were going to be killed and covered in horseshit, I'm glad it was Mr. Big Mouth. Were you there when he tried to hit on my wife, with me less than twenty feet away? I swear to God, these assholes think they can just do and say whatever the fuck they want without any repercussions, right? I for one am happy somebody settled his hash once and for all. Fucking right-wing scumbag. Now if you'll excuse me, I need to grab some coffee and some of this bacon." He gave Vivien a quick and totally charming smile showing perfect white teeth and turned his back to her to focus on pouring coffee.

Lenny came down the stairs, and Vivien pulled him aside, moving towards the front door. "Is that…?" asked Lenny.

"Tom," said Vivien as she lowered her voice. "Charming and attractive Tom, who is a bit of a flirt not at all distressed that Samuels is dead."

"Well no surprise there, the man insulted everybody he made contact with. What's our next move?" asked Lenny.

"There is still one county that's yet to be heard from," said Vivien, remembering a phrase an Irish police sergeant from Wisconsin used to use.

Right on cue the lone traveler came slowly down the stairs, moving as if he was nursing a sore knee. He was wearing black jeans and a tight black t-shirt that revealed hours spent in the gym. Vivien and Lenny watched him silently and continued looking at him as he stepped d into the room.

"Hello…" he said uncertainly as they both stared at him. "Everything okay?" Vivien studied his face, which was a rectangular, handsome rendition of a man in his 40's, or maybe early 50's. It was hard to tell because his hair and fashionable goatee were completely gray. His voice was soft and he stood in a natural, non-defensive posture.

"Not really," said Vivien. "A man was killed last night. The man I saw you arguing with at the front desk yesterday. Would you mind telling us your name and where you were last night?"

The guy looked away, breaking eye contact for a second, and then looked back at Vivien. "Wow. Are you guys cops or something?"

"Not exactly," said Lenny, "just concerned citizens. And Viv, before you scare the bejesus out of him, I can tell you his name is Vince, he lives in Washington and he's an architect. Isn't that right, Vince?"

"All quite correct," said Vince. "So the guy I was arguing with, the obnoxious newscaster guy. He's dead? Dead here in the building? How?"

Vivien gave Lenny a quick look, once again amazed by his ability to instantly ingratiate himself with anybody within his reach, and a bit peeved that he'd stepped in and interrupted her interview procedure.

"Actually we found him in the barn, dead, along with his car. Did you hurt your knee or something, Vince?" asked Vivien. "I noticed you limping a bit coming down the stairs."

Vince tapped his thigh with his hand and said, "Leg cramp. That bed is way too soft. So, you found him dead in the barn this morning. Are the cops coming?"

"Yes they are," said Vivien. "And in the meantime everybody needs to stay put and stay out of the barn. I don't suppose you saw Samuels anytime after you had the argument, did you Vince?"

Vince's face went grim as he said, "No, I did not. What a jerk. I'm actually not surprised somebody killed him. Got any suspects?"

Vivien looked at him evenly and said, "Yep. A whole building full of them."

Chapter 9

Mooky stood at the window looking out to where she wanted to go. There was more to do in the building where the large animal lived. There were smells to explore and things to see, but she needed to get out of this room for any of that to happen. She watched out the window to see if anybody was going to the building, or to see if Vivien had left her alone. She could feel vibrations in the floor and had heard voices downstairs, but now the voices had stopped. The house was quiet except for the sound of the rain that was soft but constant.

Suddenly the door opened and it was Vivien. Mooky wagged her beautiful tail back and forth at the sight of her and went to give her a big sniff to see where she'd been and if there were any other dogs about. Vivien gave her head a pet and said, "Watch out Mooky, mama needs her gun." Mooky didn't know what most of those words meant, as Vivien reached for her shoulder bag and pulled out a plastic box.

She opened the box and Mooky saw the snapping metal thing that smelled like oil and smoke. Mooky didn't like that thing as it made harsh noises when Vivien played with it. Vivien took one piece of the thing and slid it into the other piece as it snapped together. Mooky perked up her ears and watched as Vivien pulled a piece of it back which made it snap again.

Mooky wanted to leave the room and enter the time of go. She wanted to go out. She wanted to go out and go to the building with the big animal. She wanted to see the animal and find out what was out there. She looked at the door to the room and it was open. Vivien was now poking at her phone, talking into it and trying to make it talk back. Mooky didn't want to leave Vivien but she wanted to go out. She walked quietly to the door and looked out, showing Vivien that this was where she wanted to go, but Vivien wasn't paying attention.

The smells of food were drifting up from downstairs and Mooky hadn't eaten breakfast yet. She walked through the door, looked down the hall for the other dogs but didn't see any of them, so she turned and headed down the stairs.

She got to the room where the front door was and could smell the food coming from the other room. She ignored the food and went to the door, pressing her nose against the crack, smelling the rain and the wet grass and the other dogs and the large animal in the building. She stood there a moment, her tail moving slowly so that anybody who saw her would know that's where she wanted to go.

She heard a noise behind her and turned to see a man walking towards her. She thought she had seen the man the other day but wasn't sure if it was the same man. She pointed her nose at him, opened her mouth a little bit and sniffed to see what he smelled like. He got closer and he was not afraid of her. He was a friendly man. He said, "Hey, whatcha doing? You need to go out or something?"

Mooky perked up her ears and gave the man all of her attention because this was exactly what she wanted. Her tail swooped faster as she knew this was the time of go and she was going to get to go out. She barked a soft "woof," to let the man know that he was right. He was coming closer and she nuzzled his leg to get a good smell. He didn't smell like any of the dogs in the house as his hand went to the doorknob and pulled it halfway open.

"Is your master out there? I don't know if you're allowed out there by yourself. Let's take a look, huh?"

He had a piece of meat in his hand and the smell was strong, especially since Mooky hadn't had her breakfast yet. She tried to ignore it as she moved against the man's leg, and now her nose touched the screen door and she pushed and the door opened and she was out. Out in the time of go and trotting across the porch and now onto the wet grass.

She heard the man yell, "Hey, wait a second…" She didn't know what those words meant and she didn't know the man but she did know where the building was and now she ran for it, her nose pulling her back to where she had been earlier.

She ran to the building, ignoring the spots where the other dogs had been. She went to the big door but it was closed and she wanted to go inside.

She ran in a circle around the building, stopping to pee and sniff, then moving on, looking for another way in and finding a small door in the back that was cracked open.
She stuck her nose in the crack and pushed and the door came open. It was dark in the barn but she went in, smelling for the animal and detecting all types of other smells. People had been in here, the animal was back in the corner of the building, and there was a trace of the most magical smell of all.

It was a smell that she had smelled before and could not resist. It was the smell of decay and food and fear all rolled into one smell that cut through all the other smells. She worked the floor of the building looking for the source, trying to find the right direction. The smell was all around her and yet was nowhere.

She sniffed and stopped when she heard voices coming towards her. She heard Vivien calling her but she went back to work sniffing around the walls, around the posts, following a trail that stopped, then started again, then vanished.

She caught a faint whiff of something else, something she recognized. It could be a collar or a leash or a wallet. Something that smelled thick and musky and now she saw it on the floor, half-hidden by hay and now it belonged to her. It was a stick but an odd-looking stick and she had found it, so the stick was hers.

She picked the stick up in her mouth and headed for the door because now it was time to play, 'Get the Thing.' She had the thing and now everybody would have to chase her to try and Get the Thing. But first they would have to catch her.

She came through the door and she had to tilt her head to get the stick outside with her. Now she was out in the time of go. It was raining and Mooky could see Vivien and Lenny and Buddy coming towards her and that meant the game was on.

She dug her claws into the cool wet earth as her tail stretched out straight behind her. She ran towards Vivien, playfully growling and chewing on the stick that made it move so they could all see that she had the thing. She had the thing and they would have to get it. Buddy saw the thing and began chasing her, running beside her as he tried to grab it. She stopped and changed direction, now heading way out into the green field. She could hear Vivien behind her telling her to come.

She was not ready for the game to be over but she ran back towards them, teasing them so they could see the thing and see that it was hers. Vivien's voice had changed and Mooky could tell that she was being bad and if she continued she might not get to go. She ran towards Vivien and Lenny as Buddy came running up beside her. Vivien said, "Mooky, you sit. Sit right now and drop it, right now."

Mooky did not want to sit but she would drop the thing and dare them to try and pick it up before she could grab it again. She worked her jaws and dropped the stick on the ground in front of her. She looked at Vivien to show that she was a good dog and did as she was asked, while also watching to see if anybody would try to grab the stick.

"Is that what I think it is?" asked Vivien.

"It sure looks like it," said Lenny.

Mooky did not know what those words meant as they all stood there looking at the thing lying in the cool, wet grass.

Chapter 10

Vivien bent down and took a closer look at what her dog had just dropped in the grass. She was aware without looking that Lenny's head was hovering right next to hers.

"Riding crop?" he asked.

"Yep."

"The same one that Tom had?"

"Sure looks like it."

"Which can only mean that the charming Tom or the lovely Amy was in the barn fairly recently, unless Mooky found it out here in the grass."

"No, I saw her coming out of the barn with it in her mouth. Of course we are assuming it's the same riding crop."

"Right, I'm guessing they all kind of look the same."

Vivien again pulled out the hanky Lenny had given her earlier and picked the crop up, turning her body away from the dogs so they wouldn't be tempted to leap for it. They began walking back towards the house with the dogs, ducking their heads in an ineffectual attempt to avoid the pelting rain. They ducked inside the front door, trying to shake off the water and keep the dogs out of the kitchen.

"I'll put them upstairs," said Lenny.

Vivien was taking a closer look at the crop just as Tom waked out of the kitchen with a half-eaten strip of bacon in his hand.

"Hey, you found it. Where was it?"

He walked towards Vivien, extending his hand, but Vivien dropped her arm and turned her body so the crop was out of reach.

"My dog found it out in the barn. Are you missing yours?"

"Yeah, I haven't seen it since we unpacked. Let me have it."

"It's evidence, Tom. A man was killed in the barn. You didn't lose this in the barn did you?"

Vivien noticed a change in Tom's face as a wave of darkness washed over him.

"Look, lady, I just told you, I haven't seen it since we unpacked. Stop playing cops and robbers and hand it over. You're not in charge here, okay? I don't give a shit who or what you were in your previous lifetime, hand over my property and we can all get on with our lives, okay?"

Tom took half a step towards Vivien as her hand instinctively went to the gun in the back of her jeans. She rested the heel of her hand against it and debated whether she should pull it out. She was not a police officer. She had no jurisdiction here, or anywhere. She was becoming overly involved but she couldn't stop herself. She turned farther, keeping her body between Tom and the crop.

Tom stood up to his full height and said, "What is your fucking problem anyway? Fucking cops, right? Think you rule the world or something, right? Well, let me tell you something, lady—"

"Tom!" a voice cried from the top of the stairs and Vivien felt a slight wave of relief to see Amy coming rapidly down the steps.

"What the hell is going on?" she said as she stepped in between them.

"She's got your riding crop behind her back. Her stupid dog had it or something. Now she's telling me it's evidence. Total bullshit, lady. Give it back!"

"Okay, let's calm down," said Amy as she put up her hands to keep them separated. Vivien hadn't moved, but she was feeling a bit angry with Tom calling her dog "stupid." She pushed the insult out of her mind and forced herself to relax.

"Do you have our crop?" asked Amy.

"I have a crop that was found in the barn by my dog, who, by the way, is not stupid," said Vivien.

"May we have it back?" asked Amy.

"No, you may not. First of all, it may not be yours. Second of all, it may be evidence, so I would prefer to hang onto it until the sheriff arrives. If he says you can have it back, then you get it back. But in the meantime, Amy, I'd like to ask you a question."

Amy folded her slender arms in front of her, squared her stance and said, "And what might that be?"

"Were you in the barn anytime before you showed up this morning? As in, last night?"

Amy's eyes had been locked onto Vivien's but they suddenly darted away for a second as Vivien finished the question. She knew from some of her old interrogation training that breaking eye contact could be an indication of lying.

"Tell you what, Vivien. It is Vivien, right?" said Amy. "You hold on to the crop. I'll verify that ours is missing and when the sheriff gets here, the real sheriff, we'll get this all sorted out, okay? In the meantime, leave us out of your criminal investigation. Come on, Tom."

She pulled his shirtsleeve and they both turned and walked slowly up the stairs. Vivien looked up and realized that Lenny had been standing at the top of the stairs, listening to the exchange. He gave them both a tight smile as they squeezed by him and disappeared down the hall. Lenny came down and looked at Vivien with a face full of curiosity.

"Well, the plot has certainly thickened up a bit, hasn't it?"

"Like a soup turning to stew, Lenny. Come on, I need coffee," said Vivien.

They walked into the dining room and helped themselves to the buffet. Vivien poured herself a cup of coffee, loading it down with cream and sugar. She found a bear claw pastry that looked fresh, grabbed some bacon, half an English muffin, a piece of cantaloupe, and a spoonful of scrambled eggs. Lenny fussed about with a cup of tea, and then joined her at the table with a handful of cookies out of a tin.

"Cookies for breakfast, Doctor? What would your mother say?"

"If you had ever had the pleasure of meeting her, I'm sure you would know that she would disapprove, as she did with virtually everything I attempted."

"Ouch, really? I'm sorry."

"Oh don't be, it's hardly your fault. What about yours, would she allow such a thing to go on?"

For a second Vivien tapped into a fuzzy memory of eating pizzelles in the kitchen of her childhood.

Her mother baked and cooked, as many of the old-school Eastern European second-generation immigrant wives and mothers did. She could remember using a medieval-looking hand grinder that clamped onto the side of the counter. They used it to grind walnuts for cookies called nut horns, and for making their own sausage.

"She probably would," said Vivien. "Eating just about anything at any time was encouraged, hence the hips and thighs that I now still have."

"Oh stop, you look fine."

Vivien smirked at the compliment. As they started to eat, Svetlana appeared behind them dressed in a white serving jacket and checkered chef pants, gliding silently into the room to freshen the offerings.

"Meanwhile, where are we?" said Lenny. "So far we maybe have Amy or Tom in the barn with the riding crop."

"Actually, no," said Vivien. "Technically, we have a riding crop found in a barn by a black lab, and two suspects that are not cooperating with our investigation," said Vivien as she spooned in some eggs and washed it down with hot coffee. "Wow," she said, "is it just me or does everything always taste better out in the country, even simple things like eggs and coffee?" She turned and noticed Svetlana behind her and said, "This is really good, Svetlana. By the way, did you notice anything unusual last night out near the barn, or maybe hear anything unusual?"

Svetlana stopped moving and looked at Vivien like she was trying to remember something. "Big storm, lady. I hear much booming and thunder, yes?"

"Booming and thunder, yes. Maybe that explains why nobody heard a gunshot —assuming he was actually shot in the barn."

Lenny took a bite of cookie and pointed up at the ceiling. "That's right, I wonder if anybody did hear anything or if everybody assumed it was lightning."

"Well, I didn't hear anything, you didn't hear anything, Wayne didn't, and Rachel didn't – or if they did, they're not saying anything."

Svetlana picked up some empty plates and disappeared through a swinging door back into the kitchen.

"What is it that detectives always talk about in the movies? Motive, opportunity, and what is the third thing?" asked Lenny.

"Means," said Vivien.

"Means, right. So I guess everybody here had a motive, right? I mean, the guy was such a total douche bag everybody wanted to strangle him."

"Right, but is being obnoxious enough of a reason to kill somebody? I think we should be thinking beyond his personality. Was it a crime of passion, a bizarre accident, perhaps, or something more premeditated?" asked Vivien.

Chapter 11

Vivien had no answer to her own question but she did have some facts to consider regarding the possibility of premeditation. The only one in the group who knew the dead man before they arrived at the inn was Rachel. She pulled a sweet, sticky corner off the bear claw and popped it into her mouth as Lenny announced he was going to his room to check on his dog.

Vivien handed him the riding crop, using the hanky to keep their fingerprints off it, and told him to hide it somewhere in his room. She chewed the warm, sweet pastry and tried to wrap her mind around the strange relationship that Rachel seemed to have with the now deceased Michael Samuels. She appeared to be his colleague, fielding phone calls and running interference, but she has also noticed they were sharing the same room, which would indicate something beyond professional.

Wasn't it unethical to sleep with a fellow employee, even in the TV business? And why had she refused to believe Vivien about finding the body of her dead employer? She had no motivation to lie about that. None of it made much sense. She finished her meal, drained the coffee, and picked up her plate, carrying it back into the kitchen. She came through the swinging door and expected to see Svetlana at the sink, but the room was empty and the back door was standing open.

Vivien detected the unmistakable odor of cigarette smoke and walked towards the back door. The sound of unrelenting rain became louder as Vivien looked out and saw Svetlana standing on the porch with her back turned, looking out towards the barn. She had stripped off her white serving jacket and was wearing a gray, tight tank top underneath which revealed her tight, wiry frame.

Vivien could easily imagine her as a gymnast flipping herself over parallel bars in the Olympics. Svetlana was unaware of her presence and held one hand up with a lit cigarette poised near her mouth. Vivien stepped onto the concrete floor of the porch and stood perfectly still, watching for a few seconds as Svetlana slowly brought the cigarette to her lips, inhaled and then blew out a thick cloud of white smoke which hung in the damp, heavy air protected by the roof over the small back porch.

"You maybe want more eggs, new lady?" said Svetlana, without turning around. Vivien felt herself jump as she tried to fathom how she'd been detected and how the girl knew it was her.

"Oh no, I'm fine. I just brought my plate in for you and saw the door standing open. I didn't realize there was a back porch."

Vivien looked around the porch and saw a couple of large, industrial-sized trash cans in the corner, a few mismatched chairs, and a spool of twine tucked into the far corner.

"Well now you know, huh?" Svetlana flicked the cigarette out into the yard without looking to see where it went and quickly turned to face Vivien.

"Only thing is, not really available to guests. Front porch much better. Back porch for garbage. Sometimes animals get into garbage. Front porch better, new lady, okay?"

Svetlana reached for her serving jacket and whipped it around her in one motion as she stepped closer to Vivien, smiling in an odd way, like she was selling something.

"Oh that's no problem. I'm sure you're right, the front porch has a better view, no doubt. Except, you know, you can see the barn from out here pretty well."

Svetlana shrugged. "Barn, sure, everybody can see a barn, right? Barn here, barn over there, barns all around. You want more coffee, new lady? I make the fresh pot."

"Oh, no," said Vivien, as she began backing up towards the door, "too much makes me jumpy. I may actually go lie down for a few minutes, all this rain makes me sleepy, but thanks anyway, it was really good."

"No problem," said Svetlana as Vivien listened to the girl's accent. She almost sounded Russian or something. "I make it for you, special blend, yes?"

"No, I'm fine, really," said Vivien. "I'm going to my room now, but thanks…"

Vivien stepped back inside the kitchen and headed upstairs to check on her dog and figure out her next move – assuming she had a move to make. She reached the top of the stairs and walked down the hall, past her room, and past Lenny's. She wondered if the place used to be some kind of boarding house, or if they had added on to it to squeeze three more bedrooms and bathrooms out of it. She walked down the hall past the room where she'd seen Vince going into and past the room Rachel and Samuels had been in. She stopped, and listened, but she didn't know what she was listening for. Sounds of life? A body being dragged around or being dismembered? Was Rachel still in there?

Another sound caught her ear and she instinctively moved towards it. It sounded like human flesh being struck. She got up on the balls of her feet, checked behind her and walked another two steps closer towards what had to be Amy and Tom's room. She could hear muffled voices and maybe somebody asking for something, or pleading. She had serious doubts about getting any closer. If anybody stepped into the hall at this point, she would have a hard time explaining what she was doing.

She looked behind her again. Vince could step out, Rachel could step out, and here she was. What would she say? Was she lost? Checking out the door trim?

This time she heard it plain as day. A slap. Open hand, or maybe an implement hitting flesh, and now more of the pleading. Her hand went to the small of her back as she once again reassured herself that the weapon was still there. She looked at the door. Wood frame, latch lock and a deadbolt. She wondered if she still had the strength to kick in a door. It was really about the technique and knowing where to kick, but still – it had been a while.

She crouched lower, and took another step closer, controlling her breathing and going over her options. Was Tom beating his wife on the other side of the door? Were they both killing Rachel? Was her mind out of control? *Slap!* Even louder this time. She lowered her head closer to the door. Now the voices were louder. They had changed positions or something because she could hear them more clearly. She squared her position to the door and looked for the weakest place to kick.

"Is that what you want?" asked Amy, "because it's certainly what you deserve."

Whack!

It sounded like Tom cried out in pain, then said, "Yes, please. I know I did it, please give me… Ahhhh shit!"

Another blow fell as Vivien tried to make sense of what she was hearing. Amy was apparently beating Tom. What the hell? She relaxed her position and then smiled as things became a bit clearer. Some kind of weird sex thing, maybe. And here she was listening in. She smiled, took a deep breath and took a step back, thinking she was retracing her steps but a floorboard creaked and she thought she heard a muffled bark. Damn! The noises in the room stopped and Vivien spun on her heel, tiptoeing quickly back to her end of the hall.

One dog started barking, then another one, and now Mooky was barking too. She grabbed her doorknob and turned, hoping against hope that she had left the door unlocked. She had not. The knob turned but the door remained closed by the deadbolt. She fumbled for her key as she now heard activity inside the other rooms. She found the key, slid it into the lock, opened the door, pushed Mooky out of the way, got inside and closed the door behind her. She was breathing heavily. "Oh my god," she panted. She sat on the bed, petted Mooky and strained to hear what, if anything, she had stirred up. There were no peepholes in the door so she couldn't see out, and if anybody were to have seen her, they would have had to actually open the door.

She pulled the gun out of her jeans and put it back into the locked case. She fluffed her hair, put a hand to her head as if she had a fever, controlled her breathing and lay back on the bed, coaxing Mooky to come up and lie next to her. "Who are these crazy people, Mooky, and how did we get mixed up in this?" The rain provided a soothing, white noise background as Vivien settled into the warm, soft bed. She didn't get under the covers but just lay on top and let her mind wander. She pictured Amy smacking Tom. Was that what the riding crop was for? Did they have another one in there?

She was starting to feel overwhelmed by everything and for a moment she didn't want to be in a fluffy bed in a charming bed and breakfast with a dead man somewhere on the premises. She just wanted to be a normal person with a normal life – just to see what that felt like again. She thought about her mother, dead now over three years, and about the roller-coaster ride she had been on since the funeral.

Her life was not turning out the way she thought it would. She hadn't planned on injuring her back and retiring early from the only job she ever loved. She hadn't planned on her mother dying. She hadn't planned on her own retreat from the world into her house and the borderline hoarding behavior she had exhibited for a while. She was a person who liked control and things to make sense. When they didn't she reacted by trying to put things right. She knew that now and she knew that sometimes even after trying to fix things, things were still going to be screwed up, like the perfect weekend in the mountains with her best friend and her dog.

Before she could do anything about it, tears welled up in her eyes as her hand went to her mouth. She looked out the window and wept; she wasn't even sure why she was crying. She buried her hand in Mooky's thick collar of fur and cried until she fell asleep.

Chapter 12

Mooky lay on the bed next to Vivien and wondered when it would be time to eat. She was in a different location, filled with new sounds and new smells, but she knew that by now it was past time to eat. Eating was a good thing and she was a good dog. She'd been outside and found a funny stick. Because she found the stick it belonged to her but she did not know where her stick was. She could not smell it from where she was. She could smell Vivien and the leftovers from breakfast and that made her think of food again and her wonderful tail began to thump against the bed as she thought about eating.

A noise from down the hall caused her ears to stand up as her head came up off the bed. Vivien wasn't moving so Mooky jumped off the bed and went to the door. Her nose pressed against the crack, as she smelled for who was out there and what they were doing. She whined softly as she could smell Buddy and Lenny next door. There were other smells coming from down the hall; another dog and more people.

She heard a door open and close as she went to a guarding position, standing in front of the door, ears up tuned for any sound, and tail straight down ready to move forward if she had to. She stood by the door and smelled somebody coming down the hall. The footsteps were light and there was no dog. The person passed by the door and she could hear them going down the steps and the front door opening. She left her position at the door and went to the window, using her nose to push the drapes aside. She looked out, scanning from the front of the house to the back to see who it was and where they were going. She wanted to go out, she wanted to eat breakfast, she wanted to see the other dogs, she wanted to see the big animal in the barn. She started to whine and her tail started to wag. Then she saw it.

A person near the front of the house, a person outside where she wanted to be. She barked a greeting to tell the person she wanted to go. She wanted to be in the time of go. Now was the time of go and she wanted to be there. She barked again, louder this time, and she heard another dog bark. It was Buddy, next door!

And now another dog barked and the barking got louder as they barked to each other and to the person who was outside, walking around the house. The person had something in her hand and was looking for something. Mooky barked more to tell her where she was. The person below looked nervous and uncertain and now Mooky barked a warning about this person and she saw movement from across the room that caused her to bark louder and faster.

"What?" said Vivien. "What are you barking at? Be quiet!"

Mooky didn't know what any of those words meant and it didn't matter because there was danger near. She barked and looked out the window to show Vivien where the danger was. Vivien came over, looked out the window and said, "Oh my god, it's Rachel." Vivien put her shoes on and grabbed the metal snapping thing from the box where it lived. Mooky got right behind Vivien and followed her out the door. Vivien said, "No! You stay here," but Mooky could tell that she didn't mean it and now they were both on the stairs, coming down, and the door was opening and Mooky was outside in the time of go. She ran to the corner of the house, nose working the air to find where the person went. She followed the scent around the house and found her pulling on a wire that was connected to the house. Mooky barked a warning to tell Vivien that she'd found the person.

The person turned towards her and waved her arm, trying to scare Mooky, who ducked but wasn't scared. She saw Vivien coming around the house, carrying the snapping thing in one hand and yelling, "Stop, Rachel! Stop what you're doing! Drop the knife."

Mooky did not know what those words meant but now it didn't matter because she could smell that smell again. Something old and familiar and quite irresistible. Something that came from over by the barn, a smell that she could not ignore or refuse. The smell was more compelling than breakfast or anything else. She turned her head towards the smell, put her nose to the ground and headed towards the barn, following the scent.

Chapter 13

Vivien stood outdoors in the rain, to the side of the building, pointing her pistol at Rachel's hoody-clad back. The unusual and highly opinionated workmate of the dead man was attempting to cut through the phone line to the house with a steak knife. From this range, Vivien felt confident that if Rachel turned and came at her with the knife she could take her down with one well-placed shot.

She wasn't really a threat at this point, so she lowered her aim towards Rachel's leg. The Sig Sauer P220 pistol was loaded with .45 caliber rounds. A shot to the extremities could easily shatter bones, and if she hit a major vein or artery it would make a big enough hole to cause the victim to bleed out in a few minutes. Vivien did not want to kill Rachel, nor did she want to be stabbed with a steak knife.

"Stop, Rachel, that landline is our last connection with the outside world."

Rachel continued to work the knife and held out her other hand towards Vivien saying, "Hang on, I'm just about finished here," as she used the serrated edge to saw through the tiny copper wires that were already poking through the slice in the insulation.

"Rachel, please stop what you're doing or I'll have to use force," said Vivien. Rachel once again gave her a wave; the universal sign for 'go away.'   "Nobody needs to know what's going on here till Michael gets back from wherever he's run off to. He's having the last laugh, I guarantee you."

Vivien lowered the gun and quietly stepped closer to Rachel, noticing her posture and how her weight was distributed. She was leaning hard on the right leg, which was straight; the left was in front of her and slightly bent.

Vivien judged the distance, pivoted sideways and kicked the back of Rachel's knee. Rachel wasn't expecting it and collapsed on the ground. Vivien stepped on the wrist of the hand that was holding the knife, and then brought the butt of the gun down on Rachel's nose, hard enough to make her stop fighting but hopefully not hard enough to break it.

"Ufff!" moaned Rachel. The hand not holding the knife went to her face as she said, "My god, I think you've broken my nose, you fool. Why did you do that?"

"Drop the knife, Rachel, or I'll do it again," said Vivien as she stood over her and held the gun up like she was getting ready to deliver another blow.

Rachel dropped the knife and said, "Okay, okay, fine. Take the knife, alert the media, bring the press down on us. Maybe you can sell the book rights if that's what you have in mind, but get your goddamned foot off my wrist or I shall sue you into oblivion."

Vivien scooped up the knife, tucked the pistol into the back of her jeans and stood back as Rachel picked herself off the wet ground and got to her feet. She checked her hand for blood, and sniffed as her eyes began to water.

"Why are you trying to cut the phone line? Your colleague or boss or lover or whatever is dead. He's not coming back from anywhere. Why don't you believe that?" said Vivien.

Rachel straightened her hoody and said, "Well, maybe you're right and maybe you're wrong about what's happening here. But I can guarantee you it will be easier to straighten out without telling the world, especially since you have yet to produce a body. I heard you on the line to the sheriff, so the cat is already out of the bag. Why further complicate things? But what do I know, you are the former peace officer, right?"

Vivien turned to examine the phone line. Rachel had managed to cut through the insulation on the cable that exposed several tiny wires inside, some of which were also cut, some looked like they were still intact.

"Great," said Vivien. "You've done an excellent job of further isolating us from the outside world. Hopefully whoever killed him doesn't have you on his list as well."

"Show me his body, policewoman. Then maybe somebody may start to believe you," Rachel retorted.

"I'm working on that, believe me. It's only a matter of time…" Vivien glanced around and realized that Mooky had disappeared. "Oh jeez, did you see where the dog took off to?"

Rachel pointed towards the barn. "She went that way, towards the scene of the alleged crime. Maybe later she can rescue a child who has fallen down a well or something."

"Very funny, Rachel. Please don't do any more damage to the phone lines. I seriously do not understand what you hope to accomplish by trying to hide whatever is going on here."

Rachel checked her nose for blood and said, "No, no, I give up Officer. Good luck with the case," before flipping up her hoody and turning to walk back inside.

Vivien watched her go, waited till she was out of sight, and then walked around to make sure Rachel wasn't hiding behind the corner, just as she heard the front door slam shut. Vivien turned around and walked back towards the barn, squinting through the rain that had now turned into a mist that seemed to be hanging in the air as a slow-moving cloud.

She started calling her dog as she got closer to the barn, and entered the structure through the side door. Michael Samuels's beautiful white car was still parked in the middle of the barn, and Vivien noted that the horse, Zeus, was back in a stall and seemed to be keeping an eye on her. She once again marveled at the size and grace of the animal and said, "Hello, big boy, just looking for my dog." Vivien walked around to the back of the car and saw Mooky sitting on her hind legs, her nose pointed directly towards the trunk.

"What are you doing in here? Bad dog. What's got into you, you should have…"

Vivien's voice trailed off as the dots began to align in her brain. Mooky was pointing right at what could be the next twist to the case, whatever the case was. Vivien sniffed the air, and sniffed near the trunk; she couldn't smell anything unusual, but she didn't have the nose that Mooky and Zeus had. She looked from the trunk to her dog and back again.

"Sure," she said. "That makes more sense. Now we just have to find out who might have the keys. Come on Mooky, let's go eat."

She smiled as her dog's ears perked up and she came to complete attention. Vivien exited the barn, got her dog out and began walking back towards the inn when she heard the sound of an engine coming from the road into the place. She squinted into the rain and eventually recognized Wayne riding a four-wheeled ATV. Mooky began barking as he got closer. Vivien grabbed her by the collar and said "Shhh...be quiet."

Vivien waved at him and he pulled up closer. "What's going on out there, Wayne?"

He shook his head, pulled a red bandana out of his pocket and cleaned off his glasses. "Road's all washed out. Happens every time it rains hard and it will stay that way till the rain stops. What's going on in my barn?"

"Well, Rachel, the dead guy's girlfriend or whatever she is, tried to cut the phone line to the inn with a steak knife. I tried to stop her but I may have gotten there a bit too late. I also have reason to believe that the body of the dead man is in the trunk of the car in your barn. All we have to do is find out who has the keys and we'll have the killer."

Wayne looked off towards the mountains and said, "Oh really, what makes you say...wait a second. She cut the phone line?"

"Yes sir, she was trying to. I stopped her but she did manage to get halfway through it."

Wayne looked down at his muddy boots and said, "God dammit, I knew those people were trouble when they booked the room. How are we going to find out who has the key – or better yet, can't we just wait till the sheriff gets here?"

Vivien wiped some water off her forehead and said, "I would like nothing more than that, sir, but as you just mentioned, he's not going to get here till the rain stops and I am a bit concerned that we may have an armed killer amongst us. A killer who may become more desperate as the escape route remains closed, especially now with the phone most likely dead. And especially if I'm right about where the body is. I sure wish I could pop open that trunk. It might answer a lot of questions in a hurry."

"Yeah, well. I got a whole barn full of tools if that will help. Come, on let's get out of this rain."

Vivien walked back towards the inn and Wayne peeled off towards the barn to park the ATV. She came inside, and noticed Vince sitting at the table with a half-finished cup of coffee. She made a beeline towards the phone, picked up the receiver and felt a wave of relief wash over her when she heard a dial tone. She dialed the number to the sheriff's department and got a busy signal. She hung up, and said, "Well, at least it still works."

She sat down across from Vince and said, "So, did you hear any strange noises last night, Vince?"

He was slowly chewing a bagel and looked at her, saying nothing for what seemed like a long time. He finally swallowed, calmly took a sip of coffee and said, "Lots of thunder, but given the circumstances I wouldn't call that strange, would you?"

"Nothing like a gunshot coming from back by the barn?"

He shook his head and said, "Why are you playing detective here, Vivien? What do you care about any of this? Not really your business, is it?"

"A good point, sir, but since we have nothing else to do and nowhere to go, and because whoever did it is walking around with us here in the building, I'm a bit concerned they may try to cover their tracks."

"By killing a house full of innocent people? Seems kind of far-fetched, doesn't it? Besides that, who says we're stuck here? I'm getting ready to drive out of here in about an hour."

"I'm afraid you can't do that, Vince. The sheriff wants everybody to stay here; besides, Wayne was just out on his ATV and says the road is washed out. Nobody is going anywhere."

He slowly took another bite of the bagel and before he started chewing said, "Well we'll just see about that, won't we?" He cleared his throat, dropped the napkin on the table, pushed the chair back and left the room without saying another word.

Vivien put her face in her hands and breathed in, trying to reconnect some of the dots. Dead guy in the barn, then the body vanishes. Nobody likes the dead guy, but who dislikes him enough to kill him? The body is probably in the trunk, Wayne has tools they could probably use to pry it open. Rachel tried to cut the phone line, but why? What was Amy hiding? What about that weird scene with Svetlana on the back porch, what was her deal? Would Vince try to drive through a flood to get out, and if so, why? Do the dogs need to go out? What day is it? When will this rain stop? Should she try to call Will? Can bears get rabies? And where did she know Tom Stoddard from?

She heard footsteps and looked up to see Lenny looking at her with raised eyebrows.

"What?" she said.

"What are you doing?"

"Reviewing the case?"

"And?"

"I have no answers, but I'm pretty sure the body is in the trunk of the car in the barn."

"Oh? And how do we know this?"

"Mooky smells something out there. She got out, ran right to the barn and sat right behind the car, basically pointing at the trunk."

"Seems logical. Think we should pop the trunk?"

"No keys."

"Well you may not need them. I had a Beamer once and there was a button in the glove compartment you could push to open the trunk from the inside."

"What?"

"Yep. Could be a button. As I recall the door opened the last time you tried it, right?"

"That's right. We probably should at least look. I'm also a bit concerned that we're going to compromise the real investigation if the sheriff ever finishes with the rabid bear."

Lenny rubbed his chin and looked up towards the ceiling of the room. "Mm-hmm, I hear that. But let me pose this to you. Assuming the killer is one of us, do you think they would kill again to try and hide their tracks?"

"That thought has occurred to me, and Weird Rachel tried to saw through the landline with a steak knife. She got halfway through before I stopped her. Luckily the phone still works."

"What? Well, there you go. She's the one," said Lenny. "That's why she doesn't want anybody to know till she can hightail it out of here and maybe hope somebody else gets blamed for it."

"Maybe," said Vivien as she shifted in her seat. "Something still isn't right. Come on, let's go look at the car. Wayne told me he has a bunch of tools we could use to pop the trunk, if we can't find that button."

Lenny and Vivien herded the dogs into their rooms, ducked into the rain and trotted back to the barn with shoulders hunched against the weather. They came in through the side door and found Wayne, feeding the horse.

"It feels like it's never going to stop," said Vivien as she attempted to shake off the rain.

"By next week it's going to be like it never happened," said Wayne as he turned to her and put his hands on his hips. "So, what about the car?"

Vivien used the hemline of her jacket as a glove and opened the driver side door, which emitted the same whiff of fine leather upholstery. Vivien opened the glove compartment and sure enough saw a small white button. She found the hanky, pushed the button and a satisfying click announced the trunk opening. She walked to the back of the car, Vince at one side and Wayne at the other as the trunk lid majestically and slowly opened to reveal... nothing.

"Jeez oh man," said Vivien.

"Hmph," said Lenny.

Wayne scratched his head in puzzlement. He pulled a small flashlight out of his back pocket and shined it down.

"Well, there is something. Isn't that a pistol down there?"

"Where?" said Vivien as she peered in, following the light down to the deep recess of the trunk and saw, hiding in the shadows, a Glock 19.

"Ha!" she said. "Not what I was expecting but something indeed." She used to the hanky to pick the gun up and brought the muzzle to her nose, sniffing for recently ignited gunpowder.

"Anything?" said Lenny.

"Maybe. I can't really tell," she said. "Wayne, I have to tell you, I'm a bit concerned by the strange things going on here, especially since the killer is probably amongst us and maybe has plans for covering his tracks. I'm afraid you and the rest of the guests are at risk."

"I'll do you one better, little lady. This kind of thing could kill my business, if you'll pardon the pun. I'm struggling as it is. Running this country inn thing was really my wife's idea and she passed away about eighteen months ago. I'm trying to make the best of it but it's a struggle and this little episode is definitely not helping my frame of mind."

Vivien took a deeper look at Wayne and saw a man who had lived a full life, probably working the land, now trying to play the role of the happy innkeeper and maybe not that happy about the transition.

"I understand, Wayne. One of the guests, Vince, told me earlier he's planning on driving out of here in a little while. Obviously the sheriff would prefer if everybody remains here."

"Well I wouldn't worry about that, unless he has a boat or a submarine he's not going to be driving anywhere, except maybe to his own funeral."

"It's that bad?"

"The end of the road looks like a river."

"Okay, well hopefully he'll come to his senses before it's too late."

"What do we do in the meantime?"

"Sit tight," said Vivien. "We don't have much choice. I really wish we could get an internet signal, I need to do some quick research."

"You could try the computer in my office, it's on a satellite system that usually works even when the other one goes down," said Wayne.

"Lead the way," said Vivien as she got a better grip on the gun while trying not to mess up any fingerprints it might hold. "If it works we may get some answers pronto."

She followed Wayne back to the house, as Lenny announced he would go upstairs and check on the dogs. Vivien blew him a kiss and handed him her key. Wayne led her to a door in the corner of the kitchen that she'd never noticed before. He pulled a key out of his pocket, threw the bolt lock open and they stepped into a small office packed with boxes of files scattered about the floor in a haphazard style.

"Sorry about the mess, I usually don't bring guests back here," said Wayne as he picked his way around to a rolltop desk that held a surprisingly modern-looking laptop. He jabbed a finger at the space bar as it came to life, and squinted at the screen. "Where do you want to go, Google?"

"Sure," said Vivien as her eyes tried to take in the clutter. "Google is fine."

"Looks like we have a signal. Go ahead and jump on here, just let me know when you're finished. I'll be at the front desk. I'll try the sheriff again while I'm up there."

"Okay, Wayne, great." Vivien gave him a quick smile, waited till he ducked out of the room, and then sat down, laid the gun on the desk and searched for 'Tom Stoddard.'

She got an accountant in a town nearby, a wedding photographer, and an article in *The Washington Post* about a road rage incident that happened about a year ago. "Bingo," said Vivien to herself and the walls.

The article described the kind of thing that happened on a regular basis on the clogged highways around the nation's capital. Motorist number one cut off motorist number two and it led to violence. According to the article, Tom Stoddard cut off another motorist, named Anthony Jaffee, somewhere out on 66 West during the evening rush.

Jaffee then followed Stoddard for several miles and at speeds exceeding one hundred miles an hour. The two cars exited the highway deep in the exurbs and got stuck at a red light. Jaffee approached Stoddard with a pistol and fired into his car, breaking the driver side window. The shot somehow missed, Stoddard got out of the car with a hatchet-like survival device and fractured Jaffee's skull with multiple blows while horrified onlookers watched the bloody melee.

According to the article, Stoddard was an intellectual property attorney and the other motorist worked for the GSA as an administrator. The District Attorney viewed the incident as a messy case of self-defense. Stoddard walked with a warning and a promise to seek counseling. The other participant, a father of two, died from his injuries. The article linked to another earlier account of the event that showed a mug shot of Tom Stoddard, the guy who was staying upstairs and who possibly enjoyed being slapped around by his wife in the bedroom. The article made no mention of her, but that wasn't surprising.

Vivien took a deep breath and then Googled Michael Samuels, finding numerous articles quoting a variety of incendiary things he had said on air and in print. The list of people and organizations that he had insulted and/or angered over the years was quite astounding. Everybody, it seemed, had a good reason to hate him, except his employer. There were several articles in media trade magazines about how successful his show was in terms of generating big ratings and even bigger money.

Variety had been tracking his latest round of contract negotiations, chronicling a complex arrangement that, according to the most recent reports, had grown increasingly contentious. Vivien wasn't sure what it all meant but apparently his first contract was coming to an end and the network was on the hook to honor an extension that would boost his earnings even higher than the stratosphere he was currently occupying. There were quotes from Samuels where he expressed frustration with his current arrangement and hints that he might jump ship to another channel.

Most of the people in the network appeared to want to keep him, but some unnamed sources in the organization were becoming increasingly uncomfortable with his statements and wanted him gone. Vivien's eyes widened as she read a quote from an anonymous spokesman who said, 'In some ways the best thing that could happen would be for Samuels to just disappear, that would be the simplest and best solution.'

"Huh," Vivien said to herself.

She didn't know Rachel's last name, so Vivien added the name after Michael Samuels and immediately got an article quoting a 'Rachel Mitchell' regarding a fracas that happened in a bar in Georgetown involving a thrown martini glass. She Googled Rachel Mitchell and found a LinkedIn profile for her that identified her as the executive producer for Samuels' show, *The Final Word*. She'd been with the show for five years, and before that worked for Fox News, and was a graduate of Duke University. "Huh," Vivien said again.

The door to the room then opened, and Amy stepped in and closed the door behind her. "We need to talk," she said. Her eyes went from Vivien to the gun lying on the desk. Vivien used the hanky to slowly grab the gun, pulling it off the table, and putting it in her lap as she felt her shoulders instantly tense up.

"Seriously?" said Amy. "Like I'm going to grab the gun or something?"

"Well, we don't know what you're going to do, do we Amy?"

Amy sighed, pulled out a kitchen chair that was in front of the desk, moved a stack of paper off the seat and sat down.

"Well I'm not, okay? I don't even like guns. Keep your gun."

"This isn't mine. Pretty sure this belongs to the guy that was in the barn who you helped pronounce dead. Remember that? It wasn't that long ago."

Amy narrowed her eyes at Vivien and said, "Sure, I remember."

"That's good," said Vivien, "because since then the body has gone missing and now some of our fellow travelers don't believe it ever existed."

"But you and I know better than that, right Vivien? It is Vivien, right?"

Vivien nodded and kept her hand resting lightly on the grips of the pistol. "Mm-hmm," she said, "we do."

"Okay, good, so that's what I wanted to talk to you about. See, I was in the barn before."

Vivien tried to keep the expression on her face neutral as she leaned back in her chair and said, "I see, and what were you doing out there? What happened between you and Samuels?"

"Nothing! Okay? Nothing happened. Why is it everybody thinks we were doing something?"

Amy's voice had risen and she quickly dropped her head, breaking off eye contact as she tried to contain herself.

"Sorry, it's just that Tom thinks there was something going on too. Which is ridiculous because the guy was obviously a complete jerk, but we did have kind of an exchange, in the barn last night, before we found him, you know…"

"Dead."

"Right. Dead. I didn't kill him by the way, he was very much alive when I left him."

"Nobody is accusing you, Amy. I'm just trying to keep the rest of us safe till the sheriff gets here." Vivien felt herself automatically slip into the comforting cop role and wished she had a legal pad or something to take notes. She took a quick glance around the top of the desk, saw a pen and a stack of Post-it notes, but she didn't want to do anything to distract her witness while she was talking.

"I know. I know that, okay? It's just, well, the guy said some stuff to me in the barn that was, you know, creepy. I mean, beyond creepy."

"How did it start? Why did you go out there in the first place?"

"Simple, really. One of the reasons we chose this place was because I wanted to do some riding. I went out to the barn, with my riding crop, to check out the horses. Wayne thought Zeus might be a little too big for me and was going to bring a mare over from one of the other farms. That was before all this crazy rain screwed everything up. I went out to the barn to see if the other horse was in there."

"But the other horse wasn't in there, was it?"

"No. But Mr. Asshole was. He had pulled his car in because he was afraid birds were going to crap on it or something. Anyway, when I walked in he was already in there, fiddling with something in the trunk, and well, it started."

"What started?"

"You know, the usual. He starts hitting on me, wants to know how long I've been married. Am I happy? Regular stupid guy stuff."

"So what did you do?"

Amy's eyes narrowed and her voice came up again. "What do you think I did? I blew him off of course. I told him to drop dead, get a life, etcetera, etcetera. I mean, what a total jerk, right?" She took a breath, calmed herself again and went on.

"Anyway, I'm checking out Zeus. I brought an apple for him and I'm trying to get him to eat it, and Mr. Douche Bag steps out of view, right? Like he's now hiding behind one of the other stalls or something. I can't see him anymore and I'm thinking, good, maybe he left or dropped dead."

Amy stopped like she was trying to remember something, or perhaps deciding whether she should go on.

"Is there more?" asked Vivien.

"Oh, yeah, there's more," said Amy. "So anyway, I can't see him. I'm petting the horse and he starts to call to me across the barn. He's saying, 'Amy, come here I want to show you something...' You know, stuff like that. I'm ignoring the idiot of course, God knows what's on his mind but he won't stop, right? I mean he's just really bugging me. So against my better judgment, I start to walk down to the other end of the barn because he's still saying this stuff except now he's getting, you know, dirty about it."

"What do you mean, dirty?" asked Vivien as she felt her lips getting dry.

"You know, he's talking about what he wants to do to me and how he's going to do it nice and slow and he wants to do it with Tom watching, I mean some really sick stuff, right?"

"Right," said Vivien. "Very sick."

"So anyway I walk down there, really quietly, and I know I'm close, I can tell by his voice, and I peek around the stall and there he is, pants down, going to town."

"Going to town?"

"Masturbating, Vivien, jacking the monkey, whatever they call it."

"Oh god," said Vivien. "What did you do?"

"Well, he sees me, right? So now he's walking toward me with his hand still, you know, hard at work, and he's coming at me like he's going to grab me or something, so I let him have it with the crop."

"Let him have it?"

"Yep, right across the face, and I scream something like, 'you pervert.' I'm so upset I drop the crop and run back inside the inn."

"Then what?"

"Then nothing. I come back outside in the morning and run into you guys and the asshole is dead. End of story."

"Why didn't you tell me this before, Amy? This would have cleared up some questions."

Amy looked down at the hardwood floor, scratched and stained from years of use. "I know. I should have. But I was embarrassed, you know? I mean the whole thing really creeped me out."

"Sure," said Vivien, "I certainly understand how it would."

"Good, I'm glad we got this straightened out."

Amy stood up and put the pile of files back on the seat as she flipped her hair and said, "Oh, and Tom and I are probably going to try and get out of here later today, turns out he has a friend who's going to be in Washington tomorrow and we're going to drive back."

"I'm not sure that's a good idea, Amy. The sheriff wants everybody to stay put, and besides, Wayne says the road is basically washed out."

"Yeah, I know but we really need to get back. I'm pretty sure there's more than one way back to civilization, probably including a few that Wayne doesn't know about."

Vivien's hand gripped the gun a bit tighter and she wondered if it was loaded. She used to carry a Glock when she was on the force in Milwaukee and she could usually tell from the weight whether the magazine was loaded or not, but that was a long time ago and she wasn't sure.

"I would advise against that, Amy, but obviously there's nothing I can do to stop you."

Amy looked at her with a face that showed no emotion and said, "Good, Vivien. I'm glad we understand each other." She turned and left the room.

Vivien found an empty plastic grocery bag on the floor by the desk and put the pistol inside. She picked her way around the clutter back to the door and left the room, headed for the front desk. Wayne was standing behind it, going through an unopened stack of mail. He gave her a quick look and said, "Find out what you needed to know?"

"I think so. At least for now. Thanks for letting me do that. Amy and Vince have now both told me they're going to try and drive out of here today. Do you think that's even possible?"

He put down the mail and said, "Tell you what, except for the time when I was in the service I've lived my whole life within twenty miles of this house. When it rains like this, the road to the south gets cut off by that little creek that runs under it, except it's not a little creek right now. You can't even see where the bridge is when it's like this, and even if you could see it, the current would pull you downstream in a second."

"How about if you go the other way?"

"That's actually worse because it runs up towards the mountains. There's one place where you might get across but the next crossing will be deeper and you run the risk of getting stuck between the two of them. If you look out to the horizon you'll see a line of mountains. Well, this spot we're sitting in is the low part of the valley that all this rain is draining into. Once it stops raining, the creeks and rivers will start to draw back to their normal levels, but as long as it keeps raining like this, we aren't going anywhere."

Vivien heard a noise and Lenny appeared in front of her with an expectant look on his face. "I think the doggies need to go for a little walk and some breafkast. They're getting kind of antsy."

"Okay, I need to get out of here myself for a few minutes. Want to brave the weather and take them out?" asked Vivien.

"I have a couple of raincoats ya'll can borrow," said Wayne.

"Let's do that," said Lenny.

While they fed the dogs, Wayne disappeared for a few minutes and came back with two large yellow raincoats with built-in hoods. "They don't look very stylish but they'll keep the water off you, and there's umbrellas in the stand by the door."

"Perfect," said Vivien. After Vivien hid the Glock in her room they donned the coats, herded the dogs out the door and started walking back towards the road. Even with all the explanations, Vivien was still curious about how bad things really were. The skies were a solid flannel of gray and the rain remained a constant deluge.

"So did the computer work?" asked Lenny.

"Oh, it works all right. So Tom, Amy's husband, killed a guy with a hatchet."

"What?"

"Yep. I knew I'd seen that name somewhere. It was a road rage incident a few months back. He and another motorist got into it, they pulled over, the other guy had a gun and Tom whacked him, literally, with one of those survival hammer-hatchet things."

"Oh my god."

"Yep, and not only that, Rachel is in fact the producer of Samuels' show, which kind of makes her the boss. Apparently, Samuels was in some kind of contract negotiation with the network that nobody was really happy about."

"Wow," said Lenny. "So it was probably Tom, right? He's got a mean streak. Or do you think it's Rachel?"

"I don't know. The other thing is, while I was in there, Amy comes in and tells me she and Samuels had a run-in in the barn earlier in the evening."

"A run-in. What does that mean?"

"Apparently he, um, dropped his pants and was, well, you know..."

"Showing her things?"

"Right. Showing her things. Do you think that was his whole problem? Like maybe he was, you know, frustrated and had to act out to get everybody's attention all the time?"

Lenny adjusted the hood on his raincoat as they followed the driveway out towards the road while the dogs ran out ahead of them. "Well I don't know the man well enough to make any kind of diagnosis. I can tell you that men prone to indecent exposure are usually much younger than our departed news anchor. The technical term is 'exhibitionism', but I don't think that was his problem. I think he was just, you know, seizing the moment as it were." They both giggled a bit at Lenny's joke as they swished forward in the long, wet coats, their feet making sucking sounds in the wet ground.

"So is it safe to say that Amy was not amused with his advances?"

"She was not. She says she hit him with the riding crop and that's how it got in the barn. Apparently, she likes carrying it around."

"Hit him and left?"

"Hit it and quit," said Vivien, which caused her to giggle some more.

"So, he shows it to her, probably says something to her; she hits him, drops the crop, leaves the scene and he's still in there and alive doing whatever," said Lenny.

"So she says. There are a couple of things bothering me about her story. She says she went to check out the horse. Horse stays in the stall, Samuels drops his pants, says some stuff, yanks the crank, takes a blow and yet we find him in the stall behind the horse, pants down, shot in the head. Plus she says he was calling her name from behind the stall, was acting creepy, and yet she walks down to where he's at, by herself, and has a look."

"She probably would have just run away, right? Why didn't she just leave?" said Lenny.

Vivien shuddered under the raincoat and looked at her friend. "Doesn't quite ring true, does it?"

They stopped and looked at where the small bridge leading into the property had been. There was now a river, 100 feet wide, stretching across the road, bridge, and adjacent fields.

"Holy smokes," said Vivien, "he wasn't kidding about the road."

Lenny squinted into the rain, pulled at the hood, and said, "Nope. He sure wasn't. You'd need good-sized boat to get across that. But getting back to the barn, it sure seems like we're missing a few pieces to the puzzle, aren't we?"

"It does indeed. Quite a few pieces, I think. I can't imagine why Samuels, pants on or off, would get into the stall with the horse, can you?"

"Well, Viv, darling... speaking of odd sexual practices, it's not totally unheard of for humans to, well, you know...engage with members of the animal kingdom."

"Oh my God," said Vivien. "Do you really think that's what happened?"

"I'm not saying it did, I'm just saying it could. I mean maybe it was all perfectly innocent and he was back there just admiring old Zeus from behind."

Vivien pursed her lips together and squinted towards the mountains, imagining gallons and gallons of rain washing down the hills, all coming right to this little bridge. "I'm thinking maybe somebody moved the horse. Maybe moved the horse temporarily and then moved him back after Samuels did whatever he was doing in the back of the stall."

Lenny pointed his index finger up towards the wet heavens. "Ahhh a mucking operation gone bad, perhaps?"

"A what?"

"Mucking," said Lenny. "That's the word horse people use to describe the process of cleaning out a stall. So your theory has some validity. Perhaps another person enters the barn to tidy up things for Zeus. The horse is led out, something-something happens in the back of the stall, and then the horse is led back in."

"Right," said Vivien. "So who is our mysterious mucker?"

"Who indeed? It would have to be somebody who knows horses and had the authority to move the horse."

"Well, that's only Wayne, isn't it?" asked Lenny

"As far as we know," said Vivien, "Come on, let's go find him."

Chapter 14

Vivien and Lenny turned the dogs around and headed back towards the house. They got inside, toweled them off and put them in their rooms. They came back downstairs and found Wayne at the front desk doing paperwork.

"Did ya'll go down to the road?" asked Wayne.

"We got as far as the bridge," said Vivien.

He looked at them for a second, made a face of consternation, and said, "Bad, isn't it?"

"Yeah, I can't imagine anybody driving out of here anytime soon, especially if you say going the other way is worse," said Vivien. "So Wayne, let me ask you something. Were you in the barn the night Tom died?"

He hesitated a second and then looked right at Vivien and chuckled. "Well I wondered when your investigation was going to get around to me. After all, I didn't like that fella either. In fact, I may have said something to you that I would now regret. But to answer your question, no. I wasn't in the barn. Why are you asking?"

"Well sir, I'm toying with the theory that somebody moved the horse out of his stall and then back into it at some point."

"Like if somebody came out to muck the stall," added Lenny.

Wayne's eyes moved from Lenny's face to Vivien's and back. "Oh, yeah, well sure. That's an easy one. Svetlana takes care of the horses. That's part of why I hired her. She can ride, train, take care of the tack, and she does muck the stalls, so yeah. I'd say she's the one you want to talk to."

"Is she around?" asked Vivien.

"Oh, she's always around. She lives on the premises. She's got a little apartment in the basement. More like a dungeon. I tried to get her to take the small room in the attic, but she liked the basement better. Want me to see if she's down there?"

"Would you mind?"

"I don't mind, be right back..."

As Wayne left, Lenny and Vivien traded looks as Lenny mouthed the word, "dungeon," and made a mock-terrified face, which caused Vivien to laugh out loud. After a few minutes Wayne came back and said, "Okay, she's down there. Follow me." They walked into the kitchen as he opened another door that Vivien hadn't noticed before.

Wayne yelled, "Okay, Lana, they're coming down..." He then turned to Vivien and said, "I call her Lana, it saves some time."

"Sure," said Vivien. "Thanks Wayne."

Vivien and Lenny picked their way down the narrow steps that must have been carpeted several years ago from the worn condition of the fabric. The air smelled a bit musty as they reached the bottom of the stairs. A washer and dryer were on one wall, along with an old-fashioned stationary tub. The rest of the space was configured like a low-ceilinged apartment. There was a full-sized bed in one corner, a small kitchenette with a sink, stove, and an apartment-sized refrigerator.

They could see the door to a bathroom, which had a chin-up bar wedged into the doorframe. Svetlana was hanging by the bar, casually pulling herself up and down with no apparent effort. There was a 25-inch console TV complete with a set of rabbit ears on the top. Vivien felt like she had taken a trip in time back to her college years, or a visit to one of her first apartments. She counted Svetlana doing five more pull-ups before she stopped, settled back to the floor and turned to face them. She wasn't even breathing hard.

Vivien took a few steps closer to her as Lenny kind of hovered in the room, looking at the titles of books that were neatly stacked on pieces of furniture scattered around the room. She wondered if maybe she should have had Lenny remain upstairs, but it was too late to ask him to leave without it looking weird.

"Wow," said Vivien, "you're in great shape."

Svetlana faced her, picked up a towel that was lying on a chair, and dabbed at her forehead. "Yes new lady, is good to be strong like whip. Why are you come to visit me?"

Vivien collected her thoughts and said, "Yes, well. I… I mean we, my associate and I, were wondering if you were in the barn last night, and if you saw Mr. Samuels in there while you were attending to the horse."

Svetlana tossed the towel on the couch and squinted at Vivien. "You mean Mr. No Pants Man?"

Vivien laughed nervously and looked at Lenny, who was now leafing through a book in his hand, and gave her a smirk.

"Right, he may have not been wearing any pants. He was actually killed last night. Did you know that, Svetlana? Did you see him in the barn and was he still alive?"

Svetlana squared her shoulders and reset her feet, as she looked right into Vivien's eyes. "I see him. Mr. No Pants Man was alive, but not polite. He say many things. Even horse was offended, I think."

"Yes, well that doesn't surprise me. He seemed to specialize in being rude to people. Can you just tell me what happened when you saw him?"

Svetlana looked away for a second and then took a seat on the couch, which seemed to engulf her tiny frame. She put her hands behind her head and leaned back. "Are you police, new lady?"

Vivien quickly looked at Lenny and then back at Svetlana. "Well, no, I used to be police but I'm really just trying to find out what happened until the real police get here. I'm concerned that we all may be in danger."

"Not from Mr. No Pants Man," said Svetlana.

"No, not from him, because he's… well. Anyway. What happened when you went out to the barn? Can you just tell me that?"

Svetlana exhaled and looked like she was trying to weigh her words carefully before speaking. "Okay, new lady. I come to the barn to feed horse and clean stall. Man is in there getting something out of his shiny car. I move horse to feed him and clean stall. Man starts to talk to me, telling me things he wants to do. I tell him I am only working here, no time for his games to play.

He talks and talks, saying bad things. I tell him be quiet now. He wants me to make him be quiet now."

Svetlana stopped and stared into her lap.

"So what happened, Svetlana? What did you do?" asked Vivien.

She remained silent for several more seconds, and then glanced up at Vivien with a hard look on her face. "I need to keep this job for a while, new lady. I did nothing illegal to man. He takes his pants down and starts to come near me. I tell him, stop. No."

"I understand. Nothing is going to happen to you, especially if it was self-defense. Do you understand? Did you feel like your life was in danger?"

"Yes, maybe he's a raper, maybe killer, I don't know. He comes close still talking. He's playing downstairs; he's closer all the time. He has belt looped around his neck. Very odd, this No Pants Man. I tell him, no. I see escape zone for me is the door behind." Svetlana stopped and looked back at Vivien, like that was the end of the story.

"Wait. I don't understand. What escape zone? Did he touch you? Did you just run out the back door? What happened?" asked Vivien.

Svetlana dropped her head and stared into her lap. "Wayne a good man. A good boss. Wayne hire me to help run things, especially in the barn."

"Yes, I understand that, Svetlana. Look, I know you don't want to get in trouble and I don't want you to get in trouble. But I need to know what happened out there. You didn't shoot Mr. No Pants Man, right? Was there a struggle? What was he doing with the belt? Was he conscious when you left the barn? What happened?"

"No," Svetlana said. "No guns, no shooting." She took a deep breath and said, "I tell you already. The belt is already around his neck. Some men, they like this when they play downstairs. I have seen this. But I don't want to play with him. I run away, I find Wayne. Wayne throw him out or call police. Goodbye, No Pants Man."

"Right, okay," said Vivien. "So you got away from him and then, what? You left to find Wayne?"

Svetlana shrugged and said, "I run back to house. I come to find Wayne, only raining now. Big thunder, much wind. Come in to find Wayne but he's not around. Then people want things. New man can't close window, new lady wants more pillows. Now busy for a while and storm blows up. I think Wayne must be in barn and so I go back out and put horse back in stall."

"You put the horse back in the stall with No Pants Man? That's what you did? Was he still alive? Was he still out there?"

"I don't see No Pants Man," said Svetlana. "I think he must be gone."

"Gone?" said Vivien. "Gone where? How long were you gone?"

"Maybe ten minutes, maybe more. Maybe he leave, but he's gone either way."

"And then what? What did you do then?"

Svetlana shrugged and said, "Then nothing. I finish barn work, I come in the house get ready for breakfast, next day."

Vivien sat there and studied Svetlana's face, but she saw nothing suspicious or even interesting about the expression. It told her nothing. She didn't think Svetlana was lying but she couldn't tell if she was speaking the complete truth either. It was a blank.

"Okay," said Vivien. "Thanks, Svetlana. Are you ready, Lenny?"

"Yes, of course," said Lenny. "So nice of you to let us come down and speak to you. I am curious about one thing before we leave, if I may ask?"

Svetlana shrugged again, the thin shoulders jumping up and then settling back in a gesture of acquiescence.

Lenny cocked his head and looked at her like a dog hearing a strange sound. "When you were out there in the barn by yourself, and he was coming after you without his pants on, were you frightened at all? I mean, he was kind of an intimidating person."

Svetlana squinted at Lenny, and smiled, the first show of emotion Vivien had seen since she met her.

"I know this kind of man. He's big talker and no walker. Wants to be controlled by others. I could have made him do bad things as I know this type but best to keep job and stay in America."

"Right," said Lenny. "Of course it is and I'm sure you're right. Okay, I'm ready Viv." They both gave Svetlana quick, tight smiles and then picked their way back up the basement steps. They reached the kitchen, which was unoccupied, and Lenny, half under his breath, said, "So what do you think?"

Vivien looked at him and said, "I think she's mostly telling the truth. She probably did just run away. The belt thing still seems weird to me."

"Well, it's a pretty popular fetish. Choking to increase the intensity of an orgasm. Something about the oxygen shortage, but yeah, I think you're right. She doesn't seem like the crazy killer type."

"Cool as a cucumber, isn't she?" said Vivien. "If she did do it she's sure not nervous about getting caught. And how do you know about this choking thing? Where do you get this stuff anyway, Lenny?"

Lenny put his hand over his heart, bowed slightly and said, "Well I am a doctor of psychology you know, and a student of the human condition."

Vivien couldn't help but giggle. "Of course you are. I keep forgetting that."

"So what's our next move?"

"Rachel," said Vivien. "I want to talk to Rachel again."

The walked back through the kitchen and found Wayne back at the front desk doing paperwork.

"Thanks for that, Wayne. It was helpful," said Vivien.

"No problem. Did she tell you what you wanted to know?"

"Yes," said Vivien. "She was very helpful. We're now wondering if you can confirm which room Rachel is in. I think I saw them go into the last one down the hall."

"Well, actually I can't do that, legally, but I can go upstairs and see if she'll see you. Privacy concerns, you understand?"

"Yes, of course," said Vivien.

"Plus, she may not want to talk to you, since you punched her in the nose."

"It wasn't really a punch, Wayne, and she was armed with a steak knife."

"I understand. I'm just saying she may not want to talk to you."

"Well, please ask, won't you? It may help us find out what happened to her friend."

Wayne nodded, put his pen down, and headed upstairs.

Lenny half-whispered, "Pretty sure they were in the big suite at the end of the hall."

Vivien said, "I know, but I don't want Wayne to think I've been up there spying and figuring out where everybody is staying."

Wayne came back and said, "Go on up, she's in room 1, but she says you can't take your gun in with you."

"That's fine," said Vivien as she lifted the denim shirt she was wearing over her t-shirt to reveal the top of her jeans. "I'm not armed."

Lenny and Vivien climbed the stairs, went to the end of the hall, and Vivien knocked lightly on the door.

"Enter," a voice answered.

Rachel was lying on the bed, with her arms crossed, barefoot, still wearing the black jeans and the hoody she had on when she had tried to cut the phone line. Vivien approached the bed and looked at Rachel's nose, which bore a small cut. One of her eyes had started to turn black. "Looks like you're going to get a nice shiner, Rachel."

"If there's permanent damage you will be hearing from my lawyer, I can assure you," she said in a cool, dry monotone. "Now, how can I help you?"

"Yeah, well that would certainly be your right, just make sure you tell your legal team that you were armed with a knife at the time."

"I meant you no harm, *Officer*."

Vivien sat down on a side chair as Lenny hovered by the door. She noticed the room was at least one and a half times larger than hers. "Be that as it may, I did warn you. You were engaged in an act of vandalism. You were armed and acting irrationally."

"According to you."

"Yes. According to me. So listen, I was able to get an internet signal and did some research on you and your boss."

"How fascinating," said Rachel. "And what did your research reveal?"

"It revealed that you produce the Michael's show and that there was some kind of contract renewal process going on at the network."

Rachel arched an eyebrow and said, "Gee, no fooling. I told you about hat earlier. Did it say where Michael has run off to as he plays out this little game?"

"No, it didn't, but I'm glad you mentioned that because my sources weren't really clear on exactly who is on which side in terms of what the network wants, and how a disappearance could affect his business partners. Would you be some kind of beneficiary if he were dead?"

Rachel stared at her in silence for several seconds, like she was trying to figure something out, and then suddenly burst out in a loud, infectious cackle of a laugh.

"Oh I get it. You think I killed him for, what, some kind of insurance settlement? And then tried to cut the phone line to cover my tracks? Is that your deduction Sherlock? Please..."

"Are you saying that's not what happened?" asked Vivien.

Rachel took a deep breath and rubbed her face in frustration. "Let's try this again, shall we? Michael and I are not married, *Detective*, or whatever you are, so there would be no beneficiary relationship, okay? My attempt to sever the phone line was an attempt to avoid a lot of embarrassment and media hoo-ha over another Michael Samuels disappearance story that isn't really a story."

"Another disappearance story?" said Vivien. "What does that mean exactly?"

Rachel went silent and looked evenly at Vivien. "Look. This really isn't any of your business but Michael has, well, let's call them mental health challenges, okay? Things we don't want any press on. There have been incidents in the past where he kind of just checks out for a few days. I'm assuming that's what's happened here, despite what you claim to have seen in the barn, okay? As you have discovered in your little investigation, I am his producer, so naturally I have a keen interest in what the world knows and does not know about Michael's whereabouts until I know his whereabouts. All righty?" Rachel finished and looked at Vivien with a cocked eyebrow.

Vivien cleared her throat and squared up her shoulders a bit. "Sure, Rachel. I know you don't believe me about what I saw, or maybe you don't want to believe me. I don't understand all this big time Hollywood dealmaking. I'm just a retired law enforcement official from a small town in the Midwest, but something sure smells fishy here."

"An excellent choice of words, Vivien. If you are correct and he is in fact dead, the smell of the decaying corpse will certainly help us locate him, correct? If and when that happens I will be more than happy to cooperate with you to resolve this matter expeditiously. But until we have a body I would ask you to respect our privacy and keep this under your hat until the real police arrive, which should be when, by the way?"

"As soon as they catch the rabid bear," said Vivien.

"Fine. As soon as they catch the rabid bear. In the meantime I promise to stay away from the phone line if you promise to not tell anybody else what may or may not be going on here, deal?"

Vivien thought for a second and said, "Deal," feeling like they had come to an agreement. She got up as gracefully as she could and nodded at Lenny, indicating the show was over.

They exited the room on little cat feet and closed the door very quietly. Vivien motioned Lenny to follow her and they tiptoed back down the hallway to her room.

She unlocked the door, greeted her very happy dog, and sat on the bed while Lenny slipped into a side chair and petted Mooky.

"So, what do you make of that whole scene?" asked Lenny.

"Something doesn't sound right with her story," said Vivien. "I'm not buying it."

"I'll say. But do you get the feeling they are boyfriend slash girlfriend in addition to whatever this professional relationship is?"

"Well, they were apparently sharing a room, and there's only one bed in there," said Vivien.

"Right. But they didn't seem to like each other that much. Maybe that's just the kind of relationship they had. What do we do next?"

"I still need to talk to Tom – alone, preferably, and I sure would like to know what happened to the body." Vivien snapped her fingers as Mooky looked at her, left Lenny's grasp and walked towards her, with her tail slowly wagging back and forth.

"Where's that body, Mooky?" said Vivien. "What has happened to old Michael Samuels, huh?"

Chapter 15

Mooky stood by the front door and spun in circles, catching glimpses of her beautiful tail as it flashed by her nose and then disappeared. She was very excited and very much wanted to go outside because Vivien had told her that now was the time of go.

She could hear the rain outside the door dripping onto the roof, falling onto the roof and making puddles. She knew the ground would be cool and soft against her feet as she touched her nose to the doorknob, telling everybody that this was where she wanted to go.

Vivien was there, and the man who smelled like the house, and Lenny, and the woman who stayed with the man she did not like. This woman smelled like fruit and flowers and she was not afraid. They were all standing next to the door and talking, saying words that Mooky didn't understand.

She felt footsteps and saw two more people coming. Her ears stood up and she sniffed the air for a dog, and then saw the dog. He tail swooped and she pulled at the leash, trying to get closer to the dog for a better smell but she was being held in place.

"So, is this the body-hunting posse?" said the woman with the dog.

Vivien said, "I'm not comfortable calling it a posse, Amy. But yes, we are going to walk the dogs around the property and see if we can locate the remains of Michael Samuels, to put an end to the speculation regarding whether he is deceased or not."

"Well I think that's an excellent idea and I would like to volunteer Keisha's services as well, as she has an excellent nose."

"I have no objections to that," said Vivien. "I would only ask that you keep her on a leash. You, Tom, me, and Lenny can take the lead, Wayne and Rachel can stay behind us. Even though it's only been twelve hours or so, the dogs may be able to give us a clue. Mooky has actually found human remains before so I'm confident we're going to solve this part of the mystery right here and now."

Mooky's ears shot up when she heard her name mentioned and her tail thumped against the wall. She whined and pulled at the leash, bumped Buddy with her nose and wedged herself tighter against the door. Nobody was entering into the time of go without her. She was very excited and wanted to go right now. There was more talking and more words she didn't understand until Vivien said, "Okay, everybody ready? Let's go..."

And now the door was being opened and Mooky could smell the rain and the earth and the barn and the animal in the barn and that very special smell that she could not refuse. She needed to find where that smell led and now they were outside and she was following the smell to the barn. Vivien was trying to slow her down but she could not help herself; she pulled at the leash and barked, telling everybody about the smell and where it was. Buddy was next to her and the other dog too. They all knew about the smell and they were all going to find where it was coming from.

They got to the barn and worked around it to the door and went inside and the smell was everywhere. It was in the car and under the car and in the room where the animal was. The animal snorted and stomped its foot and Mooky could feel the ground move. She looked under the car and around the car and the smell was everywhere and nowhere. It was strong and then it was gone and she jumped and barked because the smell was in the sky. She turned in circles trying to figure out how to go to the sky because this is where the smell was coming from. She pulled Vivien to the wall of the house and barked and looked up telling everybody that the smell was up there. They all seemed confused and now Buddy and the other dog went to other parts of the barn trying to figure out how to go up to the sky.

Chapter 16

Vivien could feel perspiration on her forehead as frustration was quickly taking the place of excitement. She was finally on an active hunt for Michael Samuels's body with a semi-organized group of her fellow travelers. As soon as they found the body everybody would believe her and they could move beyond the silliness of doubt. She could silence her own small voice of uncertainty and resume the active investigation and find a path back to normalcy. But now her dog was barking at a wall in the barn, Buddy, the Portuguese Water Dog, was peeing on a wall, and Keisha the spaniel was looking like she wanted to roll around in horse manure.

"Well," said Amy. "What now?"

Rachel was standing off to the side, arms folded, looking very disinterested and at the same time somewhat vindicated by the dogs' failure to locate the dead body. Lenny was staring out the barn door scratching his head, Tom was staring at the horse, and Wayne had picked up a broom and was randomly moving piles of straw and dirt around.

Vivien wiped her hand across her forehead, looked at the wall and her dog, who was now sniffing along the edge of the wall where it met the ground. She tried to make herself solve the puzzle. She kicked the wall lightly and tried to force herself to think logically, like an investigator; like the police officer she used to be.

She'd never made it into the upper echelon as a detective. Her career was cut short by a back injury sustained in a training exercise. The pain sometimes came back in damp weather like this and she realized that, for whatever reason, it hadn't been bothering her. Her mind was drifting, she needed to focus.

These people were counting on her. Why had she put herself in this situation? This was supposed to be a mini-vacation. They hadn't looked at one antique. They hadn't taken one long walk with the dogs. Instead, she was hanging out in a cold damp barn on a wild goose chase for a body that even she was beginning to doubt she'd seen.

She stared at the wall. The wood was rough-hewn and looked positively ancient. She ignored the insistent Amy watching her every move. She forgot about the doubtful Rachel, standing arms-crossed in a defensive position. There was a slight rumble of thunder and she saw Wayne look briefly up at the ceiling. His gaze shifted to Tom, who did the same thing.

"Is there a way up to the hayloft, Wayne?"

"What?" said Wayne.

Vivien walked back out to the center of the barn, looked up and studied the semi-open platform that comprised the barn's second story.

"The hayloft, isn't that what you call it? Is there a way up there?"

"Used to be a ladder, but it broke and I haven't gotten around to fixing it, so I use this aluminum one."

He gestured at a paint-splattered aluminum ladder stuck in the corner, which Vivien hadn't noticed before.

"You think the asshole climbed a ladder before he croaked?" said Tom with a bit of barely-disguised malice in his voice.

"I can assure you he was deceased when I saw him in the stall," said Vivien as she found a bit of confidence hiding inside her psyche. "Mind if I take a look up there, Wayne?"

Wayne shrugged and said, "Suit yourself. Just be careful, there's no railings and the floor is a little shaky up there..."

He went to the corner and grabbed the ladder as Svetlana walked through the barn door. "Now is a party in the barn, yes? She said."

"I'm not sure it's much of a party," said Wayne as he moved the ladder into position. "Are you sure you want to go up there ma'am?"

"You'll fall and break your neck, then we will have a body to deal with," said Tom as he watched her with arms crossed.

"Shut up Tom, I saw it," said Amy. "No idea how it could have flown upstairs but it has to be somewhere."

"Upstairs not safe, new lady," said Svetlana as she too watched with arms crossed.

Vivien looked at Mooky again as her dog's tail swooped back and forth and her nose snuffled at the earth where it met the side of the barn. She wondered if she was about to make a fool of herself in front of these strangers, then quickly decided she didn't care. She was going up and trusting her instincts. Wayne reached into his back pocket and pulled out a small flashlight. He handed it to Vivien, looked her in the eye and said, "I'll hold the ladder for you, ma'am."

Vivien said, "Thanks Wayne," tucked the flashlight into the front pocket of her jeans and began climbing the ladder, rung by rung, making certain she had a good grip before pulling herself up the next step. The air felt a bit warmer as she went up, and she noticed it smelled slightly different. It was less like mud, horse, and earth as she ascended and more like dust and hay and something else. At first she thought it was her imagination, a small optimistic hope that she was right and that this was not a futile gesture but the hope was gradually edged out by the revulsion triggered by the smell of cologne. She stepped off the last rung, sliding her hiking boot clad foot onto the plywood flooring of the hayloft, turned her head towards the odor, pulled the flashlight out, clicked it on and shined it onto the corpse of Michael Samuels.

"Bingo," she said.

"You see something?" said Wayne.

"What is it?" asked Tom.

"Is it him?" said Amy.

Vivien shined the light from the dead man's shoes to his head and was somewhat relieved that whoever had pulled him upstairs had also pulled his pants up.

"Yes," she said to nobody in particular, "it's him, and he's still quite dead. I'm coming down."

She carefully made her way back to the ladder, feeling clumsy and overexposed as she climbed onto it and descended back to the floor of the barn. She rubbed her hands together, knocking off some dirt, and looked directly at Rachel. "Care to have a look for yourself? You can smell his cologne about halfway up, if you don't want to go all the way to the top."

Rachel glared back. "Fine," she said.

She took three confident steps towards the ladder and looked at Wayne, "Will you hold it for me?"

"I will, if you insist on doing this ma'am."

"I'm afraid I must."

Wayne re-established his grip on the ladder and Rachel began her climb. Vivien stepped over and handed her the flashlight, saying, "Here, you'll need this." Rachel took the light, jammed it into her back pocket and began to quickly climb the ladder. She didn't go up onto the platform, instead standing on the ladder and shining it around the space.

"Good lord," she said softy, and sighed. "Good night, sweet prince."

She carefully picked her way back down, handed the flashlight to Wayne and said, "Very well. I stand corrected. What now, Sergeant Friday?"

Vivien looked around at the group and then back up towards the hayloft, focusing on a pulley that she had noticed before. In her mind she reviewed a piece of trivia, maybe from a high school math class, about how a pulley helped reduce the amount of effort needed to move a heavy object. Somebody had obviously moved the body into the hayloft, but even with the pulley it had to be somebody with enough physical strength to do it, and there was still the question of why.

"I think we need to try to contact the sheriff again," said Vivien. "I think we need to make sure that nobody tries to leave here, for their own personal safety and because somebody in this group killed Michael Samuels and then tried to hide the body for reasons unknown. Then I think we should have a group meeting where everybody can share information on what's happened here."

"Agreed," said Lenny.

Chapter 17

Vivien led the group back towards the farmhouse and wondered again how there could be any rain left in the sky as it continued to drizzle. They ducked inside the front door as she turned to them and said, "I would like everyone, including Wayne and Svetlana, to meet in the kitchen in fifteen minutes so we can go over a few things. Wayne, I need Vince there too, if you would be so kind to knock on his door and invite him. In the meantime, I'm going to try the sheriff's office again."

The group broke up as Vivien went back to the landline, read the number on the sticker and punched it in.

"Sheriff's office." It was the same old lady voice that answered before.

"Yes, this is Vivien Szabo out at Wayne's bed and breakfast again, calling about our, um, issue here. Is the sheriff back yet?"

"Hold please."

Vivien held the line and could hear the crackle of the police radio in the background, which took her immediately back to her days on Milwaukee Metro and the Secret Service. She wondered what the chances were of her leaving law enforcement and being involved in a second mysterious disappearance. Maybe the universe was trying to tell her something.

"This is Sheriff Olson, how can I help you?"

"Oh Sheriff, thank God. It's Vivien Szabo again, I called before about the dead body out here at Wayne's B&B."

"Right, sorry I haven't gotten back to you. Some lady on the other side of the county thought she saw a bear, turned out to be the neighbor's cocker spaniel. Anyway, did the body come back?"

"Yes sir, I'm afraid it has. It's currently in the hayloft in Wayne's barn."

The line went silent again for a second and Vivien knew she sounded like a crazy person.

Another crazy person seeing things that weren't there, like a bear that was actually a dog.

"Well for a dead man, he sure gets around, doesn't he?"

"Yes, well, I know it sounds weird, but..."

"Let me ask you a question, ma'am. Anybody else out there see him? The body, I mean."

"Yes," said Vivien, "two other guests have seen it."

"Has Wayne seen it?"

"Well, no. Not technically."

"Is he there?"

"Yes, of course."

"Might I speak with him for a moment?"

Vivien pulled the phone away from her ear and looked towards the kitchen for Wayne. Other feelings from her career started to trickle into her consciousness. The feeling that this man on the other end of the phone wanted to talk to another man to verify what the crazy woman was saying. She tamped her irritation down and took a breath. The sheriff and Wayne obviously knew each other and presumably had for years. The sheriff was just another overworked, underpaid cop trying to do his job. This wasn't personal. This had nothing to do with her. She set the phone down and stepped towards the kitchen to look for him, just as Wayne came down the stairs.

"Vince says he'll be at the meeting. I had to talk him out of trying to drive out of here again. You city folk are a stubborn lot aren't you?"

Vivien smiled and said, "Actually I grew up in a small town in Wisconsin, but I hear what you're saying. The sheriff is on the line and wants to talk to you."

"Oh, okay," said Wayne. He put his hand on Vivien's shoulder as he brushed by and gave it a little squeeze. "'Scuse me, ma'am."

She smiled again, thinking Wayne was not a bad man but she was getting a little tired of being called ma'am. She stayed where she was, pretending to be deep in thought, as she wanted to overhear the phone call without looking too obvious.

Out of the corner of her eye, she watched Wayne pick up the phone.

"Bob? Yes, it is peculiar. Mm-hmm. No, I haven't seen it with my own eyes but three guests have, the last one while I was standing there. Okay. All right. Yep, that's fine."

He hung up the phone and came back to Vivien. "Nobody leaves until he gets here, and he can't get here till the rain stops. We're back to where we were, ma'am."

"Well at least somebody is paying attention, and Wayne?"

"Yes ma'am?"

"Please stop calling me ma'am. My name is Vivien."

"Yes ma'am. I'll work on that, Vivien."

Vivien gave him a quick smile as Lenny appeared at her side. "So where are we?" he asked.

"I'm going to go up to my room for a few minutes and collect my thoughts."

"I need to freshen up myself. Knock on the door when you're ready, but in the meantime what did the sheriff say? Is he coming out?"

"He can't until this damn rain stops, which is one of the reasons why I think we need to clear the air and keep everybody safe. I'll be down in ten minutes."

Lenny nodded as Vivien left the kitchen and headed for the stairs. She opened the door, hugged her dog and broke her own rules again by inviting Mooky up onto the bed. She lay there and her thoughts wandered. She thought about her boyfriend, Will, the cop. They'd been together for two years and although she wasn't thinking about marriage she was wondering where it was going to end up. He'd been married and divorced, and worked a grueling schedule as a homicide detective in Washington, D.C. She loved him but she had lived alone for most of her adult life and had become set in her ways. Maybe the relationship was in a fine spot right where it was.

She pulled out her phone and just for the heck of it pushed his name to place a call that probably wasn't going to go through. She expected nothing but it actually rang and she felt her heart jump as she pulled the phone to her ear, hoping against hope.

"Where the hell have you been?" said the crackly voice on the other end.

"Oh my god, Will. You won't believe what's going on up here. It's been raining since we arrived, the phones haven't been working, and a man was killed the first night we were here."

There was silence on the other end; she pulled the phone away from her ear and looked at the screen to see if the call had been dropped. The icon still showed them connected.

"Will? Are you there? Did you hear me?"

"Yeah, I heard you. What do you mean killed, and are you okay?"

"Yes, Lenny and I are both fine. Some guy, a TV news guy who was staying here, checked in, insulted everybody and now he's dead. Shot and strangled, and the sheriff can't get out here because the road is washed out. Oh god Will, I wish you were here. These people are a bunch of weirdos. The guy who runs the place is okay but the rest of them... I just don't know what to do."

"Okay. Well, what can you do?"

"I'm trying to keep them safe but they keep talking about driving out into the storm."

"Well excuse me for saying so, ma'am, but some of them are probably trying to leave because they killed the schmuck."

"Yes, I know that, Lieutenant." Vivien smiled as they slipped back into calling each other the pet names they used when they first met. She didn't mind when Will called her ma'am, it was the regular people that bothered her.

"Maybe you should do an Agatha Christie, get them all together in a room and solve the mystery."

"You must be reading my mind, Lieutenant. My only concerns are, I've never read any Agatha Christie, I don't know who done it, and what happens if I do solve it? What if they try to fight back, or flee the scene?"

"Are you armed?"

"Yes, of course."

"Do you have any theories?"

"Kind of."

"Maybe I should come up there. How long did it take you to drive there?"

"Oh no, Will. You can't. Even if you could get off work, the roads are washed out. Isn't it raining down there?"

"A little bit. Most of it went around us and apparently it's camped out over your head. Listen, honey, I got to go but just try to take care of yourself and wait for the cavalry."

"Okay, I'll try. I love you and I miss you. This has been the worst get-away weekend I've ever had."

"I know honey. I miss you too. Hey one more thing, Agatha. Just remember these three things, means, motive, and opportunity, okay? Also, you need to outthink these bastards. You have to be crafty. Use your secret womanly powers."

"Okay Will, I will try, although I have been thinking of just chambering a round and threatening to shoot them unless they cooperate."

"Don't do that, they'll put you in jail unless you can convince everybody that you felt your life was in danger. Are any of the suspects armed?"

"I don't think so but who knows, everybody has a gun these days."

"Tell me about it. Please be careful, I'll try to call you back. Gotta go babe."

She heard the line go dead as she laid the phone over her heart and flopped back down onto the bed. She spent the next five minutes going over what she knew as fact and what she could deduce by common sense reasoning. As a law enforcement officer, she had never actually worked as a detective. Those jobs seemed to go to well-connected men and stellar officers who showed an aptitude for solving crimes. Apparently she was neither, or if she was, her superior officers never picked up on it.

She glanced at the clock and then triple-checked her gun was loaded with the safety on. She tucked it and the holster in the back of her jeans, using the clip on the holster to keep it from sliding down too far.

She kept an old set of handcuffs in the gun case as well and she slid those into her back pocket for good luck. She gave Mooky a final hug, flipped her shirttail over the weapon and went out into the hallway. She knocked on Lenny's door. He came out with a serious look on his face and a small notebook in his hand.

"Are you going to be taking notes, Dr. Watson?"

"I might, Sherlock. I just might."

They smiled at each other, descended the stairs and walked to the kitchen. So far, Wayne was the only one there.

"Are the rest of them coming?" asked Vivien.

"I assume so," said Wayne. "They all know about it. Svetlana will be here in a minute, she's watering the horse."

"Right," said Vivien, "the horse that had been moved from his regular stall permitting Samuels to occupy that space. Do you think Samuels could have, or would have, walked back into the stall with the horse in there?"

"Could have?" said Wayne. "Sure. Would he do that? I don't know. I really can't imagine why he would."

"Unless he was following somebody in there for reasons unknown to us," said Vivien.

"Yeah, I guess that could have happened. So what is your plan here, ma'am, I mean, Vivien. What are we doing at this meeting?"

"Let's hold that till the rest get here, Wayne."

Almost on cue, Svetlana came in through the back door and Vivien heard footfalls on the stairs. Rachel, Amy, Tom, and Vince shuffled into the kitchen and took up positions standing around the perimeter of the room.

"All right," said Wayne. "I believe you've gotten your wish, um Vivien. What's on your mind?"

"Right," said Vivien clearing her throat. "First things first. I talked to the sheriff earlier and, as I told you before, no one is allowed to leave the premises. Anybody who does try will be treated as a fleeing suspect."

"What does that mean?" said Tom. "Are you going to shoot us in the back? And also, refresh my memory, why are you in charge? This is Wayne's place, the last I heard."

Vivien was irritated and wondered what had happened to the friendly and charming Tom she had met when they arrived.

"It is Wayne's place, Tom, and even though I am no longer an active law enforcement officer, I am going to do everything in my power to make sure the sheriff's orders are carried out. I will use force if I have to, okay?"

"Trust me, she will," said Rachel. "I have the scar to prove it." Rachel touched the small cut where Vivien had struck her with the butt of her gun for added dramatic effect.

"And she has Samuels' gun too. Isn't that right, Vivien?" said Amy.

"Quite right, Amy. I also have my own gun and I excel in marksmanship. Moving on. Even if you wanted to leave, you cannot because the rain has washed out the road and Wayne has assured me there is no safe route."

"So he says," said Vince.

"If I say it, you can believe it's true young man," said Wayne. "I've lived here my whole life."

"Okay, fine. Vivien, now what?" asked Amy as she crossed her arms in front of her.

"I want to go over the chain of events that happened the night that Samuels was killed, as I believe the killer, or killers, is amongst us with a definite motivation to flee and cover their tracks. So Amy, let's start with your visit to the barn. Would you mind telling us all what happened this time?"

"Excuse me Viv," said Lenny, "would you mind if we went and sat around the table? I'd like to take notes and it's hard to write standing up."

Vivien gave a long, slow exhale as her investigation was interrupted, and said, "Fine. Let's go into the dining room." They all shuffled into the dining room as Vivien sat at the head of the table. Lenny took a position to her right, smiled at her, and said, "So much better, please continue…"

Wayne went to the other end as Svetlana sat next to him. Amy and Tom sat next to each other on one side as Vince took the other next to Rachel.

"So," said Vivien, "as I was saying…" She looked around the table and decided to make a quick change of plan. "Actually, Vince, let's start with you since you had a meeting with Samuels before he went to the barn. Can you tell us what that was all about?"

Vince looked at her with a blank expression and said, "How about, it's none of your fucking business, Vivien. I'll be glad to provide all the details when the real sheriff shows up, so the answers will actually mean something."

Vivien felt herself recoil slightly at the hostile response from the one guy who seemed to be somewhat normal in the group. She slowly reached behind her back, pretending to scratch her hip but then leaving her hand resting on the grip of the Sig Sauer.

"Getting ready to draw, Vivien?" asked Vince with a slight sneer on his face.

Lenny cleared his throat and said, "Let's all calm down, shall we? This is obviously a stressful situation for all of us and we need to keep things civil, all right?"

He put his hands on the table in a praying position and smiled in a benevolent way that eased Vivien's tension a bit. He was such a good friend.

"That's right," said Wayne. "As you all have noted, this is my house. I've talked to the sheriff as has Ms. Vivien here. We're all kind of stuck here and I would consider it a personal favor if ya'll would just answer her questions. I am kind of responsible for what goes on here, and if we can put some kind of a lid on it before the sheriff gets here I'd be much obliged. Besides that I am a bit curious about the goings-on, so please cooperate. If nothing else it well help pass the time. And no more bad language."

Vivien smiled at Wayne, took her hand off the gun and brought it into plain sight on the top of the table.

"Excellent point, Doctor, and thank you Wayne for the vote of confidence. After all, Vince is right. I have no authority here. None of us do. And since I'm the only one who's armed and trained in self-defense I should really just mind my own business. I mean, assuming the killer is amongst us, and there's no reason to assume anything else at this point, I'll be able to hold my own in a fair fight. You people don't seem to want any help from me, right? And none of you are armed, right? So why should I care? You're the ones who should be concerned with being shot, stabbed, or strangled in your sleep. I guess Wayne will be held responsible at some point."

"Me?" said Wayne. "What did I do?"

Vivien was purposely trying to stir the pot to see what would come to the surface, but she noted that Wayne was already reacting more strongly than she had anticipated.

"Wayne is a good man," said Svetlana. "No Pants Man was aggressing with me. No wonder it happened to him."

"She's right," said Tom. "This isn't Wayne's fault. This isn't anybody's fault. Maybe the jerk killed himself by strangling himself to death. He had the belt around his throat, right?"

"Still doesn't explain the gunshot wound, does it, Tom?" said Vivien.

"Maybe you shot him," blurted out Vince. "How do we know you're not the killer?"

"What counts is I know I didn't do it, Vince," said Vivien. "What are you trying to hide, anyway? Were you and he involved in something that went wrong that you don't want to discuss with the group? Maybe you're ashamed about something?"

Vince slammed his fist onto the table and everybody jumped at the sound. Vivien heard a muffled bark from Mooky upstairs.

"Okay, fine!" said Vince. "You are a serious psycho, lady. Just as crazy as the dead guy. Fine. What do you want to know? Yes, we had an argument over gay rights, okay? I was for them and he was against. He was a fucking asshole. I didn't kill him. What else do you want to know?"

Vivien breathed out slowly through her nose and scanned the faces around the table.

"See? That wasn't so hard was it?" she said.

"Fuck you, lady," said Vince.

"You seemed so nice when you checked in. You didn't see Samuels again that night?"

"No."

"And you weren't in the barn at all during the night?"

"No, of course not. What would I be doing in the barn?"

"I have no idea, Vince. Did you see anybody else go to the barn?"

Vince's lips tightened as he went mute.

"You didn't see anybody or hear anything unusual, did you Vince? Like a gunshot? A man was killed in the barn, Vince. If you weren't involved you would have no issue telling me because you're oh so innocent. But if you did see something or hear something and you don't say anything, you're withholding evidence, or maybe involved in a conspiracy, or maybe you're an accessory after the fact. Don't you want to do the right thing here, Vince?"

"Okay, fine. I did see her go to the barn, okay? So what? And I may have heard the gun, but who knows, there was fucking lightning all last night. Jesus. Somebody get me out of this bad cop show."

Vivien sat back and exhaled again. "Who, Vince? Who did you see?"

Vince jutted his chin at Amy. "Her. I saw Amy walking out towards the barn about 8:30. Happy now? Didn't you already know that? She already told you that, right?"

Out of the corner of her eye, Vivien noticed Amy squirming a bit in her seat. "That's right, Vince. She did tell me that. She told me she went out to the barn to check out the horse because she was planning on getting some riding in while she was here. So she goes out to the barn, with her riding crop in hand, to have a look. Anybody see Samuels follow her out there? Rachel? You two were sharing a room, you must have seen him leave, right? I mean, his car got driven into the barn at some point."

"His car was already there when I walked in," said Amy, a bit louder than she needed to be.

"Right," said Vivien. "So he went out, moved the car, then came back in, then decided to go back out to the barn? Is that what happened, Rachel?"

Rachel was staring at Vivien, tapping her fingernails on the table top in a kind of steady rhythm. She squared her shoulders and said, "That's right Vivien. He went out, moved the car, then came back in, and we had sex. Is that what you want to know? Do you want to know how we did it? I can go into more lurid details if that's what really gets you going. But after we finished, I fell asleep. I'm assuming that's when he left me and went out to the barn. Maybe to check on the car, maybe to look at the horse, maybe because he also wanted to have sex with little Ms. Amy here."

Tom slammed his fist onto the top of the table, which caused everybody to jump again, as Vivien found herself reaching for her gun. Tom said, "Now you can stop right there, Rachel. Leave Amy and your nasty comments out of this. This parlor game has gone far enough." He stood up and grabbed Amy's shoulder. "We aren't playing anymore and we're getting the hell out of here, flooded road or no flooded road."

Vivien resisted the urge to stand and draw her weapon; she remained seated, leveled her eyes at Tom, and said, "Oh come on Tom, you can see that she's trying to bait you to divert attention away from the one person who had a deep relationship with the victim and probably wanted him dead more than any of us." She looked at Rachel, who gazed back at Vivien with a benign grin. "You're actually a cunning little cunt, aren't you Vivien?"

"Language, people please," said Wayne in an authoritative voice.

Rachel gave a short nod to Wayne and said, "Perhaps I've misjudged you and underestimated your abilities, Vivien. The truth is I loved Michael Samuels despite his foibles. I have become accustomed to the rarefied air I inhabited in his presence and would not want to trade that in.

I mourn his death, so I am not the one you seek regarding his demise. I might also suggest that you are not without suspicion, despite your protests. Didn't he threaten to kill your dog? Is that motive enough to shoot somebody in dogdom? You seem quite anxious to shoot somebody. Maybe you're trying to throw suspicion everywhere except where it needs to be, hmmm...?"

"Sorry Rachel, but no. That is not motive enough for me," said Vivien. "But let's get back to what you saw, and please, leave your observations about Amy out of it."

"And what if I refuse?" asked Rachel.

"You know what? None of you have to cooperate, and actually I'm getting a little sick of it myself," said Vivien. "But aren't you the least bit curious? What else do we have to do? You don't want to play the game? Fine, go to your room and best of luck, Rachel." Vivien knew she was taking a chance and there was a good possibility they would all get up and leave. On some level, she didn't care anymore. She could sit in her room with Lenny and the dogs and wait it out. She didn't want to do that, but she could. She resigned herself to wagering on human behavior and looked at Rachel with a blank expression, indicating that she did not care what the response would be.

"Fine, Your Honor," said Rachel. "I withdraw my coarse comment, but it's entirely probable that after Michael finished...servicing me he wanted something in the trunk, his stupid gun maybe and headed back to the barn. I've no doubt the presence of the good doctor distracted him. That's the kind of man he was."

Vivien kept her eye on Tom, who was glowering at Rachel. "You really are a nasty little bitch, aren't you?" he said to her.

"I call them as I see them," said Rachel.

"Okay," said Vivien. "So Amy goes to the barn, Samuels is already out there getting something out of his trunk and confronts her. Is that right, Amy?"

Amy nodded as Vivien continued. "He makes some lewd suggestions that Amy tries to ignore. Why didn't you just leave right then, Amy? I mean, this horrible man who you don't really know says these things, and yet you stay out there long enough for him to duck out of sight briefly and then expose himself? Is that what happened?"

"Maybe that's not *exactly* what happened, Your Honor," said Rachel. "Michael was a very persuasive fellow, charming when he wanted to be, and a television personality. Maybe she was thinking about accepting the offer."

Tom shot out of his chair and lunged across the table, his hands searching for Rachel's well-toned neck. Rachel moved faster than Vivien thought possible, sliding her chair back, which caused Tom to crash face first onto the top of the table. Wayne yelled, "Hey!" as Vivien raised the gun into the air and pointed it in Tom's general direction. All the dogs in the house were now barking, as the rest of the guests sat around the table, not moving, with stunned looks on their faces.

Then Wayne stood up and put his hand on the back of Tom's neck, holding his face down on the table. He grabbed Tom's wrist and twisted his arm behind his back. "Now that's enough, young man. You will not wreck the place that Svetlana and I call home. I've had just about enough of you people."

Vivien raised an eyebrow at both the deft moves by Wayne and the inclusion of Svetlana in his words.

"If I were you, I'd calm down, Tom," said Vivien. "I think Wayne is serious. If he lets you up, can you control yourself and finish the conversation? If you can't control yourself we'll have to put some handcuffs on you." She reached into her back pocket, pulled out the cuffs, and then dangled them in front of his face. "What's it going to be?"

"No cuffs," said Tom. His voice partially muffled since his head was being held down on the tabletop. "Let me up."

"For God's sake, let him up," said Amy. "He's not going to hurt anybody. Put the gun away. This is getting way out of hand."

Vivien nodded at Wayne, who slowly eased his grip on Tom's neck and wrist.

"You're going to behave yourself and finish the conversation, right Tom?"

"Yes," said Tom. "Let me up and I'll tell you everything I know."

Vivien felt her eyebrow shoot up involuntarily; she never conceived that Tom might actually have some crucial evidence he had not revealed.

"Okay, Tom. That's great. We all want to hear your side of the story. Just grab a seat and tell us what happened."

Tom wiped his hand across his nose and said, "I know he was a jackass and that if Amy says what happened in the barn is true, you can believe it. The creep obviously had a thing for her and did what she said he did. As far as who did him in, I think maybe you should talk to little Miss Horse Whisperer over there." He jutted his chin in the general direction of Svetlana, who was sitting across from him, her wiry arms compactly folded in front of her.

Vivien felt her eyebrows shoot up again and wondered if they had always done that. She noticed that the dogs were still barking upstairs, and found it distracting. She looked at Lenny and said, "Can you go upstairs and tell Mooky she's a good girl but she needs to be quiet? Maybe if she stops, the other ones will too."

Lenny nodded, laid down his notebook and headed upstairs as Vivien turned her attention back to Tom.

"Oh really, Tom? I've already talked to Svetlana about her role in this. Is there something you want to share?"

"She was out there, okay? She's from some other country, right? She doesn't want to go back I'm sure. So maybe she hasn't told you everything. Have you, Svetlana? I'm sure she could have pulled the trigger on the prick. Couldn't you?"

Svetlana looked at Tom with an icy, blue-eyed stare. There was no way to know what was going on inside her head as she showed a mask of nothingness.

Finally she spoke, saying, "I tell new lady I was in barn when No Pants Man was talking the dirty stuff to me. He tries to come near me, I run away, and see you, Mr. Tom."

"Bullshit!" yelled Tom, and now Mooky was really going crazy, sensing the danger of the situation.

"Bullshit, bullshit, bullshit. You guys were out in the barn doing freaky stuff. I saw that, Svetlana! He still had the damn belt around his neck, okay? You fucking strangled him and you know it. Just fess up so we can put the cuffs on you and everybody can sleep tonight."

Spit was coming out of Tom's mouth and his face was red as Vivien's grip tightened on the gun.

"Don't talk to her like that, you son of a bitch, or I will take you outside and give you a lesson in manners," said Wayne.

Vivien gave Wayne a wave, trying to calm him down, and turned back to Tom.

"So, you were in the barn too, Tom?" she asked.

He turned to face her, his face a picture of rage. "You can kiss my ass too, this isn't a court of law, none of this is admissible, whether I was in the barn or not it doesn't matter. You're all a bunch of sheep letting these wolves do whatever they want. Well guess what? I'm not a fucking sheep."

Tom slowly rose to his feet as Amy looked on and grabbed his wrist. "Sit down, Tom. Don't make things worse."

Tom yanked his arm away from her. "You can go to hell, too. I've had enough of this!" Before Vivien could move to stop him or slow him down, Tom was up and moving towards the back door. He pushed Wayne out of the way as Vivien could hear the sounds of dog claws coming down the stairs. Amy screamed, "Tom! No!" as he made it to the kitchen, threw open the back door and plunged out into the darkness.

Chapter 18

Mooky was barking a warning about whatever was happening downstairs. She heard raised voices and knew it was a bad sound. She also didn't like the snapping thing, knew it was out of its box and wanted Vivien to put it away. Then Lenny came in and opened the door. She wanted to go out. She wanted to see Vivien. She wanted the snapping thing to go away and now there was shouting. She barked the warning and got around Lenny before he had a chance to put the lead on her. She ran down the hallway, slowing down to take the stairs, barking to tell everyone that there was danger near.

She reached the bottom of the stairs and could smell a cloud of fear and desperation hanging over the people in the room. She smelled Vivien and caught a glimpse of the snapping thing but then she saw movement. Somebody was running away from her and now there was only one thing to do. This person was playing Get the Thing and they were the thing to get. This was the most wonderful game of all – to chase a person trying to get away from her. She came around the table as people yelled and Vivien called her name telling her, "Stop!" and "No!"

She knew those words but she would not listen because the man was outside and running and this was the time of go. Her nails were slipping on the floor and she couldn't gain traction so she had to slow down. She could smell the man and knew he was afraid. She dropped her nose and her beautiful tail low to the ground, got through the kitchen, and felt the cool night air on her nose. She made it across the porch, down the stairs, barking to tell everybody the man was afraid and telling the man that she was coming after him to play Get the Thing. He was the thing and she was going to catch him. She could tell by his scent that he was running towards the cars and now her claws sunk easily into the wet earth.

It smelled of rain and mud and animals and wet grass and she was running, picking up speed, smelling the man getting closer with each stride. She could see a dark shadow ahead of her and was excited about catching the thing. She ran faster and lower and began growling, the sound coming out of her into the still night air, and then she jumped at the man. She opened her jaws as she leaped and then clamped them hard around the back of the man's leg. She felt her teeth sink in, the fabric and the flesh giving way as she shook her head to get a better grip.

She heard a yell from the man and felt a blow to her head as the world suddenly turned bright white. She heard herself yelp as she fell to the ground and slid on the wet grass. She rose to her feet and shook, feeling water flying from her fur. She sneezed and coughed, trying to understand what had happened, and then she saw the movement.

The man was ahead of her again and had reached the cars. She barked a warning to tell the man to stay away from the cars and stop running. She came after him as she heard the door locks pop open. The car chimed as the door opened and a light came on. She came around the open door, barked at the man and then sunk her teeth into his leg again, growling and shaking her head to improve her grip. The man was dangerous and Mooky knew now that she had to kill the thing. She bit again, tasted his blood and looked to find the man's throat but he kicked her and she yelped in pain. Her jaws released the leg as the blow knocked her backwards; she crouched, prepared to leap at the man and then launched herself at his throat, but he was too fast.

He swung his injured leg into the car and slammed the door just as she jumped. She crashed into the door and yelped again from the pain. She landed against the door and fell back to the earth as the car started. The engine was roaring right next to her head. She got up and barked as the car was put into gear, wheels spinning and making noise as the car moved backwards, slowly at first then picking up speed as the front end swung towards her. She felt the car hit her and she yelped again, feeling herself moving through the air before falling again back to the ground.

Her shoulder hurt, as she got to her feet feeling sick and unsteady. The back half of the car swung towards her as she lowered her tail and scampered out of the way. The car was moving away from her. She had learned as a puppy to never chase cars but the thing she was trying to get was driving the car. A thing that was afraid and mean and now she would chase the car forever. She heard Vivien calling her name behind her as she chased the car down the driveway. If she could not catch it, she would chase it away and now she did. It was going faster, faster than even she could run, and the smells were going away. When she could no longer see the lights on the car, she stopped running. She stood and panted as she could hear Vivien behind her, getting closer, angry and afraid.

Chapter 19

As Tom burst out the back door, Vivien was struggling to get around the table as the shocked guests ducked for cover and tried to get out of the way. While all that was going on she saw out of the corner of her eye a flash of black fur and knew that Mooky must have gotten away from Lenny, escaped the leash and was now chasing after Tom. She raised the gun to shoulder level, yelled, "Down, down, move!" as she dodged around Wayne and Rachel. She had to turn sideways to brush by them as she came through the kitchen, then the back door, then the porch just in time to see Mooky chasing down and then attempting to maul the fleeing suspect.

"Mooky!" she yelled but knew there was no way she was going to stop. The fight or flight switch in Mooky's head had been thrown and one hundred pounds of angry black Lab was now all over Tom. Vivien trotted forward, squinting into the darkness, trying to imagine getting a clear shot without hitting her dog but it was impossible. She watched Tom kick her dog in the head, which hit her like a stab in the heart. She ran faster, no longer concerned with shooting but just getting to the car. She heard the door slam, the engine started, the car was put in gear and now the front fender was bearing down on her dog.

"Mooky!" she cried again but it was too late, the car hit her and knocked her three feet backwards as Mooky yelped in pain. Vivien assumed her best friend had just been killed before her eyes as the gun came back up.

She was aiming into the back window and imagining what kind of luck she would need to blow Tom's brains out from this distance, in the dark, while shooting into a moving vehicle. It was a million to one shot. Miraculously, Mooky had survived the hit, rose to her feet to bark and just about got hit again as the rear of the car fishtailed, trying to get traction. Mooky managed to dodge the car and was now chasing it down the driveway.

"Goddammit," said Vivien as she tried to keep up. "She knows better than that." Vivien lowered the gun, broke into a trot and followed the speeding car and her running dog, hoping that Mooky would eventually stop before reaching the main road. She jogged over the small hill in the driveway and looked down towards the road just in time to see the car sliding out onto the driveway and turning right – away from the area where the river had swallowed the road. She called her dog's name again and was relieved that she had stopped running and had turned around to face her, panting, looking guilty and a little beaten up.

She reached Mooky and said, "Oh my god, oh my god. You're a very bad dog. Are you hurt? Oh Jesus Christ, you scared me." She did a quick examination, didn't see any blood, felt for broken bones, and hugged Mooky's neck as a tear rolled down her cheek. She sniffed and hugged harder, burying her face into the thick black fur. She turned her head to the right as something caught her eye. A police cruiser, lights on, siren off, was making its way down the road, slowing down to drive through the large puddle near the front of the driveway which Vivien now noticed was much smaller than the last time she was out here.

As the cruiser got closer, Vivien could read 'Luray County Sheriff's Department' on the side. It turned into the driveway as Vivien stood up and waved at the driver. The car made its way to her, the window flew down and she was looking presumably at the face of Sheriff Olson. Looking to be in his sixties, he had a round face, double chin, and bore a passing resemblance to Wilford Brimley.

"Evening ma'am. Is Wayne around?"

"Oh, my god. Sheriff, are we glad to see you. Yes. Wayne is back at the inn and the murder suspect just took off the other way. You just missed him."

"Oh really? You must be the lady I talked to on the phone, right?"

"Yes, Sheriff. I'm Vivien Szabo. But listen, we need to start pursuing; if he gets back to the interstate we'll never catch him."

"Now hold on lady, the roads are still kind of messed up, so he's not going to get very far, very fast. Get in. I'll give you a ride back to the house."

"Back to the house? Absolutely not, Sheriff. I can give you a description. I'm getting in, but we're going after him. Come on, Mooky."

She started to walk back to the rear of the car to put Mooky in the back seat but suddenly stopped.

"By the way, Sheriff, how did you get in here? Wayne told us the roads were impassable, and the last time I was out here the river was running over the road."

"Finally stopped raining ma'am. Stopped about an hour ago in the western part of the county. I told Wayne that. Things will be drying up and getting back to normal now."

"Back to normal," said Vivien as she looked up into a clear night sky absolutely filled with stars. She opened the rear door of the cruiser and coaxed Mooky inside. She sat in the front, next to the sheriff, noticed there was no computer in the car, and said, "Head out to the driveway and take a right. He's no more than five minutes ahead of us."

The sheriff made no move to do anything as the radio crackled and asked him if he had arrived on the scene. Olson methodically reached for the mic as he had for the last thirty years of being the sheriff and said, "10-4 base, at the scene and stating to investigate."

"I appreciate your thoroughness, Sheriff, but I can assure you that the man who killed Michael Samuels is at this very moment putting miles between us. I have to insist that you head out the driveway and turn right as quickly as possible."

Olson looked at her with the microphone still in hand, obviously not in a hurry to do anything.

After a few more seconds of tense silence he said, "With all due respect ma'am, I need to see the body and I also want to talk to Wayne, but I will radio ahead about the car. Did you happen to get the make, model, and license plate?"

Vivien stamped her foot on the floor of the cruiser and said, "No, Officer, I did not as he was trying to kill my dog with his car. It's a late model SUV crossover thing. Maybe a Range Rover. Look, I'll know it when I see it, trust me. You can see the body after we apprehend the suspect, now let's go."

Olson put the car in gear, which momentarily filled Vivien's heart with joy. "I wish I could, ma'am, but first things first." He pointed the car back towards the inn and said, "Show me the body, please."

Vivien fought to keep her temper in check and said, "Okay fine, but you will call it in?"

"It would be better if we knew the make and model of the car, ma'am. Is there somebody else staying here who would have that information?"

Vivien bit her tongue then said, "Yes, of course, Tom's wife probably does. I'm not sure she will cooperate but yes. The body is in the hayloft of the barn, and Amy should be back at the house since her husband left her here."

The car creeped along towards the house as Olson said, "Hmph, sounds like a real piece of work, this guy."

The sheriff pulled up next to the house just as Wayne and Amy came through the front door.

"Howdy, Wayne. Some rain huh?"

Wayne scratched his head and said, "I'll say. Did you see the guy in the SUV?"

"Just missed him apparently. Do you by any chance know the make and model of the vehicle?"

Amy said, "I do, Sheriff, but please don't hurt him. I'm sure this is some kind of mistake and he's just panicking. There's no way Tom could have killed that man. He doesn't even like guns. I'm sure this is all a horrible misunderstanding."

"That very well may be, ma'am. And who might you be?"

"I'm Amy Chan, Tom Stoddard's wife. I'm a physician, and it's a Range Rover, we bought it last year, brand new. I have the license number on the registration in my purse."

"Well all right, Dr. Chan. If you would be so kind to get that plate number I would be much obliged. In the meantime, Wayne do I have permission to take a look in your barn at the remains of the alleged victim?"

"There is nothing alleged about it, Sheriff. It's in the hayloft. You can see for yourself," said Vivien.

The Sheriff looked at Vivien and said nothing, then looked back at Wayne.

"Oh sure, Sheriff. Come on. I'll walk you back there."

Vivien, Wayne and the sheriff then walked back to the barn in a much more lackadaisical fashion than Vivien had hoped for. She watched the sheriff carefully climb the ladder as he and Wayne discussed the conditions of the roads, which included the sheriff's assessment that Tom would never make it past the East Side Bridge, whatever that was.

The sheriff reached the top, pulled a flashlight out of his pocket and shined it into the unseen darkness of the hayloft. He climbed down just as slowly and asked them, "So how did the dead man get up in the hayloft? Is that where ya'll first saw him?"

Vivien sighed a bit louder than she intended to and said, "No Sheriff. As I told you earlier on the phone, we found him in a horse stall and somebody moved the body to the hayloft."

"Probably Tom, right Sheriff? Trying to cover his tracks," said Wayne.

"I reckon that makes sense. I guess he could have used that pulley to hoist him up there, or carried him if he was strong enough," said the sheriff.

Amy walked into the barn with a piece of paper in her hand and extended it towards the sheriff. "Here you go, that's the plate number and his cell phone number. Please call him before this goes any further. He does have a bad temper and he is going to counseling for it but he's not a murderer, Sheriff."

"Well if he's not, you still have one among you then. Are there other people still in the house, I mean besides you?"

"Just Lenny, Vince, and Rachel."

"Okay, well Lenny, Vince, and Rachel are to remain where they are. I'll call in the medical examiner and have one of my deputies head out here to take statements." He glanced at the paper, put it in his pocket and said, "In the meantime I'll drive out towards the East Side Bridge and see if we can talk old Tom down off his temper."

The sheriff pulled the handheld radio out of the holster on his belt and started talking to headquarters about making all those things happen as he walked out of the barn. Vivien fell in behind him wondering if she would be able to accompany the sheriff on the pursuit. At the same time she knew there was no way he was going to allow that. She was a civilian, a strange woman who probably sounded a bit hysterical on the phone and knew nothing about the local terrain. There was no way he was going to let her go. She followed in his footsteps as they walked back towards the cruiser, Mooky trailing behind them, peeing and sniffing at the grass.

"So, did the dog go after him, when he ran to the car?" asked the sheriff.

"Yes, she did. Gave him a couple of bites too, I think. She found a human bone at our dog park back home last year."

"You don't say," said the sheriff. "Did they determine an owner for the lost bone?"

"I'm afraid so," said Vivien. "It actually led us to another set of remains that belonged to one of the dog park regulars who had been having a secret affair with one of the other regulars."

"Sounds like quite a mystery. And you helped crack the case, huh? You and your dog here?"

Vivien reached out and touched the sheriff's arm, feeling the coarse material of the heavyweight, tan-colored fabric. "Look, Sheriff. I know this all sounds like a bad TV show. But yes, Mooky and I were involved in the solving of the case – although there were still some unanswered questions."

The sheriff looked down at her hand and said, "Well there always are, aren't there?"

"I suppose," said Vivien. "The point is, I served with the U.S. Secret Service for eight years and spent another fifteen with Milwaukee Metro before that. I know what Tom looks like, what the car looks like, and have a certain feel for his state of mind."

"Which is what?"

"Angry and prone to violence, Sheriff. He has a history. There was a road rage incident awhile back. I would love to accompany you as a backup if you'll permit me."

The sheriff looked at her, his face a mask of mystery as she noticed he had blue eyes sparkling beneath the folds of aged skin.

"You would, huh?"

"Yes sir, I would."

"Are you armed?"

"Yes sir, I am."

"Can you shoot?"

"I was recruited by the Secret Service because I could speak some foreign languages and because of my expert marksmanship. I used to hunt squirrels with my uncle in Wisconsin when I was a little girl, sir."

The sheriff's eyebrows shot up and he said, "You don't say? Squirrels huh? You have to be a pretty good shot to get a squirrel. What languages?"

"Mostly Croatian, sir."

"Croatian huh? Okay, Special Agent, climb aboard and put your dog in the back seat in case we need a bloodhound."

Chapter 20

The inky black darkness of the country road was held in sharp contrast to the piercings of light coming from more stars than Vivien could ever remember seeing. The skies were absolutely clear of clouds and the warm blanket of mugginess that the rain brought had now been replaced by oxygen-rich, cool, night air. The police cruiser sliced through shallow puddles on the road and occasionally the sheriff slowed the vehicle to go around especially deep ones.

"So why do you reckon somebody wanted the dead man, dead, ma'am?"

"Please, Sheriff, call me Vivien, or Viv, or 'hey you' or anything but ma'am. But in response to your question, just about everyone at the inn had a reason to dislike Michael Samuels. He insulted an entire house full of people in a very short amount of time."

"Well insulting is one thing, um, Vivien, but is that enough to kill a man? It looked like a good piece of his head was missing from what I could see. Now that could be what you call a crime of passion, impulse kind of thing, or maybe a pre-planned assassination. Did any of the guests know him prior to their arrival?"

"Yes. Rachel. She's his producer. I caught her trying to cut the phone lines to the house because she thought I was making the whole thing up and trying to get publicity, or sell a book or something. She's very odd. I had to subdue her to get her to stop cutting."

In the light from the dashboard, Vivien saw the sheriff's eyebrow shoot up. "You don't say? It got kind of rough, did it? Do you think she could have shot him? I mean she was around him all the time, right? Where was she when the crime happened?"

Vivien's mind began replaying the facts as she knew them. She hadn't considered Rachel since nobody had seen her, or at least said they'd seen her anywhere near the barn. Had she missed something?

"She does seem to be kind of cold-blooded," said Vivien. "Nobody saw her anywhere near the barn, whereas Vince, Amy, and Svetlana were all in the vicinity and all of them had a run-in with Samuels."

"A run-in. Right. I don't know. It's not making much sense to me. Any idea where the gun came from that was used, and where it is now?"

"The gun is in my room back at the inn. It's a Glock that I saw in the possession of the victim the day before. I believe he was shot with his own gun, which we then found in the trunk of his car."

"Hmph," said the sheriff. "So somebody shoots the guy, then tries to hide the body in the hayloft and throws the murder weapon into the trunk of the victim's car. Trying to hide that too, I suppose."

"I'll admit I have more questions than answers at this point, Sheriff. The victim also had his own belt around his neck and his pants were pulled down when we found him in the back of the horse stall."

"Pants pulled down? Well that certainly is peculiar. Some kind of a weird sex thing, I reckon."

"Yes, Amy and Svetlana both claimed that Samuels was, um, masturbating, and tried to...um, approach them."

"You don't say. Well this Samuels guy does sound like a bit of a creep, maybe even an attempted rapist. Do you believe their stories?"

Vivien bit her bottom lip, which she sometimes did while thinking, and considered the possibility that the two women weren't telling the truth. Why would they do that? They had no reason to lie.

"I do, sir. I can't think of any reason why they would make something like that up, and the stories seemed similar and plausible."

"Right. Of course. Any chance either one of them could have pulled the trigger?"

"It doesn't seem likely, Sheriff, especially since we have Tom here risking life and limb to put distance between himself and the murder scene."

"Yep, unless of course he's being used as a decoy. Welp, doesn't matter at this point. First thing to do is catch up to him."

The asphalt two-lane road that they had been following around curves, through puddles and up and down hills opened onto a flat and straight stretch as Vivien watched the sheriff flip his police lights on. She felt the car accelerate and the engine roared to life.

She wondered if he had been quizzing her to justify the chase and that somehow she had passed the test issued by his cross-examination. The dotted lines of the highway flashing by bore witness to the soundness of her logic and suspicions. Maybe she was a pretty good detective after all, or maybe the sheriff had picked up speed because the road conditions had permitted it.

She looked into the back seat at Mooky who had stretched out and appeared to be sound asleep, while noticing that there was no Plexiglas shield separating the front and back seats. *Some bloodhound*, she thought to herself.

They travelled through the countryside at a high rate of speed. Vivien couldn't see the speedometer around the dash mounted shotgun but she guessed they were topping 90 miles per hour, occasionally slowing down for crossroads marked by gas stations, flea markets, and closed convenience stores. As the cruiser descended a long, steep hill, the sheriff's voice caught her off guard.

"Here's the East End Bridge, and unless I've missed my guess, here we will find our fleeing suspect." Right on cue, Vivien looked toward the bottom of the hill and saw a silver, late model Range Rover that appeared to have stalled just in front of the high water that was separating the bridge from the roadway. She could see the overhead supports of the bridge but the deck was submerged under fast-moving water.

The sheriff stopped the cruiser and turned on a hand-operated spotlight attached to the driver side door. "Welp, here's our vehicle, now where might our driver be?" Vivien scanned the area between them and the vehicle as Mooky stirred in the back seat.

"There, Sheriff. By the tree," she said as she spied what appeared to be Tom, sitting by a tree out of the water and staring into his phone.

The sheriff angled the light to where Vivien was pointing and reached for the radio microphone.

"Dispatch, we have the subject in sight on the north side of the East End Bridge. The vehicle appears to be disabled and stalled near the high water. We will attempt to engage from the cruiser."

He flipped a switch on the radio, pushed the button that lowered the window, looked at Vivien and said, "It's Tom right? That's his name?"

Vivien nodded and moved her hand instinctively towards her weapon.

The sheriff keyed the mic and said, "Tom. This is Sheriff Olson of the Luray County Sheriff's office. I'd like to ask you a few questions about what happened back there at the inn. Would you approach my vehicle please?"

At first Tom didn't move at all, and Vivien flashed on the possibility that he had shot himself, or was asleep by the tree with the phone in his hand. They waited a few seconds and the sheriff tried again.

"Your wife is concerned about you, Tom. Come on back to the cruiser so we can get this all straightened out and go home, would you, please?"

As Vivien watched, she saw Tom's head jerk towards the cruiser like he finally received one of the messages. He dipped his shoulder, rolled to his side and slowly rose to his feet. She slowly drew her weapon and tried to guess the range, making it to be about seventy yards – a tough shot in a lit, controlled environment and nearly impossible to make in this situation.

The sheriff held the mic back to his lips and said, "That's it Tom. Now you're using your head. Go ahead and turn around please and put your hands in the air so we can see that you're not armed."

Vivien watched the sheriff reach his hand to the door handle after turning off the switch that controlled the dome light of the car. He leaned to Vivien and said, "Once we determine he's not armed, let's get out slowly, keeping the doors open for cover, and see how close we can get him to the vehicle. He seems pretty rational so far."

"Right," said Vivien. "Very rational so far."

Tom complied by raising his hands, and slowly turned towards them. The sheriff made a motion to Vivien and popped his door open as quietly as possible. The moving water below them offered a soothing sound to the tense situation. Vivien followed the sheriff's lead and opened her door while also trying not to make a sound. She slid off the seat and stood behind the door as her thumb slid the safety of the pistol to the off position.

Tom was now walking towards them, limping a bit as Vivien could see where he'd been bitten on both legs. The pants were torn and a smattering of dark bloodstains was visible. Tom was mumbling something under his breath that Vivien couldn't make out. The sheriff had his hand on his gun but hadn't unsnapped the holster strap that held it in place.

In her mind, she charted Tom's distance as he got closer and strained to hear what he was saying. The sheriff raised the mic again and said, "That's great Tom, great work. Come on up here and we'll get you dried off and then we'll get this all straightened out."

"There's nothing to straighten out, Sheriff, because I didn't kill the asshole," Tom shouted. "I tried to tell everybody it wasn't me, okay? I've been through this kind of thing before and I know how it works, right? That crazy German chick is who you ought to be chasing. She fucking strangled him with his belt."

"Just keep coming forward, Tom," said the sheriff. "That's why we need you to come with us, to help us figure out what really happened. Just keep your hands where we can see them and everything is going to be fine."

Vivien gauged the range now to be fifty yards. The moon was over her left shoulder and as Tom emerged from under two large pine trees he was clearly lit and visible. Although she could shoot with either hand she was actually more accurate with her left as her dominant eye was on the left.

She shifted the pistol to her left hand and supported the wrist with her right. She checked her foot placement and slowly moved her left foot forward, turning her right foot perpendicular to her body. She noted the height of the top of the doorframe, calculating whether she could use it as a shooting platform.

"I told her I didn't do it, Sheriff, but she didn't believe me," said Tom. "She was going to put me in fucking handcuffs or shoot me or who knows what for something I didn't do, okay? I can't have another incident. So, sure. I freaked out, all right? The fucking truck stalled out before I even got to the water and now here we all are. I'll go back with you, just keep your partner there away from me, okay? She just wants to shoot somebody and it's not going to be me."

Vivien squared her hips and became aware of her own breathing as Tom slowly walked towards them. She imagined that once he got to the car the sheriff would approach him, make sure he wasn't armed, maybe cuff him and put him in the back seat of the cruiser, then they would ride back to the inn.

They would then call in the cavalry, take statements from everybody, and by tomorrow she and Lenny would be on their way back home. Maybe there would be a trial sometime in the future and she would need to come back and testify or whatever. As her mind went on a brief wander she became aware of a noise behind her, a kind of scratching and rustling sound.

She turned her head just in time to see her dog climb over the car seat. Mooky's nails at first scratched against the upholstery until her footpads got traction and suddenly she was on the ground and around Vivien.

"Oh shit," said Vivien, "Mooky, no!"

But it was too late. Mooky had decided that Tom was still a threat and was now running at top speed to intercept him.

"Hey!" said the sheriff as he reached for his gun, which got caught in the strap used to hold the trigger down.

Tom realized what was happening and saw the dark, growling blur of back fur coming right at him – again.

"Get your dog," he screamed and reached behind his back for something. Vivien crouched behind the car door and took a deep breath in, her eyes trained on Tom's moving hand. She judged the distance again: probably less than 50 feet now; noted Mooky's position and speed. When Tom's hand came back into view he was holding a pistol.

Vivien was too far away to identify the brand or caliber but it didn't matter. From this range, he could easily get a shot off that could kill her, the sheriff, or the dog. Did she feel her life was in danger? Yes, she did.

She raised the pistol and aimed for Tom's chest, the high-percentage, safe shot to take. She breathed out, moved her hand a hair to the left and squeezed the trigger. The sound of the shot cracked through the night, rising above the sound of rushing water. Her ears rang and she instantly smelled gunpowder. She was back on the target range at the police academy, and then deep in the Wisconsin woods with her uncle. There was something about that smell that triggered a flood of memories.

Tom's right shoulder jerked backwards like an invisible wire yanked it. A puff of pink-tinted vapor appeared for a second above his shoulder and then vanished as he cried out in pain.

The gun that was in his hand came flying out, spinning in the air end over end a few times until falling, unfired, to the earth. Tom toppled over backwards, landing hard and then kicking in pain. Mooky stopped her charge when the gun went off and was now sniffing and panting around Tom's feet.

Vivien looked over at the sheriff who was now holding an ancient .38 caliber police special revolver with the barrel pointed up at the night sky. He was looking at Vivien with mild disbelief on his face, his mouth hanging half open. He slowly closed it, swallowed, and said, "Squirrels, huh?"

"Yes, sir. Shot a lot of squirrels, sir."

The sheriff holstered his weapon a lot smoother than he unholstered it, walked to the trunk, pulled out a first aid kit in a waterproof plastic box, and kneeled over Tom.

"Now just try to relax Tom, looks like she barely winged you. Let me take a look and we'll call in the EMTs."

Tom had his hand over the wound as Vivien approached and grabbed Mooky by the collar. She looked down on him, looking for signs of shock, but Tom seemed alert and for the most part, unharmed.

"Well," said Tom, "are you happy, Officer Vivien? You finally got to shoot somebody, but you missed any vital organs."

Vivien looked down on him and said, "Is this your gun over here, Tom? Is this the one you used to shoot Samuels? Or is it a different one?"

"How about I didn't shoot anyone and pretty soon everybody is going to know it, and you're going to be unmasked as a fool and a lousy shot," Tom spat out.

Vivien felt her anger rising as she took a step closer to Tom, the gun still warm in her hand. "If I'd wanted to kill you Tom, we wouldn't need the sheriff's first aid kit."

"Both of you pipe down," said the sheriff, who was holding a flashlight and pulling Tom's hand away from his shoulder. "Mm-hmm, just a flesh wound as we used to say in the army. You're going to survive, Tom, hold still a second."

The sheriff squirted some kind of antiseptic onto the wound and applied a gauze pad over it. "Hold that till we get back to the inn and we can get a real doctor to look at it."

"You're taking him back to the inn?" said Vivien.

The sheriff stood up, looked her in the eye and said, "Not much choice. Only real hospital around here is Harrisonburg and it will take them 90 minutes to get here, assuming they can navigate the roads. He's not really bleeding that much but I don't want to leave him here unattended and handcuffed to a tree, so back we go. Plus I want to start taking statements from witnesses. There's an ER doc lives down the road from the inn who works for the county that I can call in for a consult."

He turned to Tom and said, "I'd prefer not to put the handcuffs on you, sir, but if you act up, I surely will pull the car over and do what's needed, is that understood?"

Tom nodded an assent, rose somewhat gingerly to his feet and walked to the cruiser. He got into the back seat on one side and watched nervously as Mooky got in the other after Vivien promised Mooky wouldn't attack him. The sheriff collected the gun, turned his lights on and headed back towards the inn. They rode back in silence as Vivien once again turned the details of the case over in her head. The sheriff got on the radio and called ahead to assess the situation. He was speaking to a deputy named Parker who was now in place at the inn and taking names and addresses down.

The sheriff keyed the mic and said, "Did you have any trouble on the roads, Parker?"

"No sir, water is pulling back quick. Still rough in the unusual places though."

"All right, very good. We have an injured party with us, got grazed with a bullet, and I'm going to have Doctor Russell come over and have a look. How many names and addresses do you have for me?"

There was a pause and Parker said, "three names and addresses so far, Sheriff, including Wayne and Svetlana."

"Roger that," said the sheriff, "we should be there in about—"

"Hold it, Sheriff," said Vivien. "He's short a name. There should be at least four."

The sheriff looked at Vivien like he was searching for a clue on her face, keyed the mic again and said, "Parker, who all do you have besides Wayne and Svetlana on your list?"

"We have an Amy Chan – the wife of the guy you have in your car – Vince somebody, and a guy named Leonard who claims to be a doctor."

"What about Rachel?" said Vivien.

"You got a Rachel, Parker?"

"Standby, sir."

Vivien could feel the back of her neck heating up; it couldn't have happened. The car was in the barn, and besides that, the keys were missing.

After what seemed like a long time, Parker came back on the radio and said, "Negative sir. No such person at this location."

"What!" said Vivien. She grabbed the sheriff's hand, pulled it to her face, squeezed the button and said, "Officer Parker, this is Vivien Szabo, Secret Service, retired. I'm assisting the sheriff with this investigation and was staying at the inn at the time of the crime. I can assure you there was such a person there. She might be in her room. Ask Wayne, he knows what she looks like."

"Um, okay, roger that, ma'am. Standby."

Again there was silence as Vivien cringed at being called ma'am, and then realized she had a death grip on the mic and the sheriff's hand was still wrapped around it.

"Sorry Sheriff," she said as she released her grip. "I got a bit carried away."

The sheriff cleared his throat and said, "Quite all right."

The radio crackled again and Parker said, "Um 10-4 Sheriff, there was a woman here named Rachel but there is no sign of her. She appears to have left the scene."

"Hah!" said Tom from the back seat. "That's what I've been trying to tell you. You're chasing the wrong person, idiot."

Chapter 21

Tom's words stung but the pain quickly dissolved into Vivien's thoughts about him being the killer. He had run, which was usually a pretty clear indication of guilt, but maybe he was telling the truth and felt like he was being falsely accused. She also cringed as she admitted to herself that his concerns about Vivien shooting him had now been realized. She felt bad about that, but not too bad as he had been reaching for a weapon. He could have easily killed her, her dog, or the sheriff from that range so she tried to push those worries off to the side and focus on the present. The cruiser was cutting through the darkness, siren off, lights on, at a high rate of speed.

Could the killer actually be Rachel? She did know the dead man the best but she also claimed to be in love with him. Vivien shook her head, reached for her phone, hit Google and felt a jolt of joy as the little wheel spun and then showed her the search screen. She searched again under Michael Samuels, Rachel's name, and Tom's and Amy's. She didn't know Vince's last name, or Wayne's or Svetlana's.

And what about Wayne and Svetlana? Was there something there she hadn't seen before? Romance maybe? She shook her head again and looked out at the inky blackness of the countryside. Fields of corn, thickets of woods, broken-down crossroads and forlorn billboards with the labels peeling off. Advertisements for local plumbers and car dealers slid silently by. She put her phone down and stole a look into the back of the car to check on Mooky, who was curled up in a ball on the seat, and Tom, who had his head back and eyes closed. She looked over at the sheriff, who had his hands at 10 and 2 on the wheel looking straight ahead.

"I think he may be right, Sheriff, as much as I hate to admit it. I think it might have been Rachel all along."

"Didn't you say you had an altercation with her?"

"She tried to cut the phone lines to the house with a steak knife and I hit her on the nose with the butt of my gun."

"Sounds like an altercation to me, and she probably had years of motivation if this guy was as much of a jerk as everybody makes him out to be."

"Oh there is no exaggeration there, he alienated everybody he came in contact with extremely quickly. I've really never seen anybody with so much hatred in their... is that a car ahead?"

Vivien had spied what appeared to be another set of headlights coming towards them, the first she'd seen since she got on board.

"Yep, looks like folks are coming out of their hidey holes and getting back to normal."

Vivien sat up in the seat, leaned forward and squinted down the ribbon of black road looking for any indication that the car could belong to one of the suspects – especially the currently missing Rachel. The headlights had an almost blue tint to them and seemed to be closing on them extremely rapidly. Vivien rubbed her eyes and said, "Sheriff, I think..."

The car was by them in a flash and Vivien pivoted in her seat trying to get a look at the rear of the car, which was a beautiful white Mercedes, the one that had been parked in Wayne's barn.

"Oh my god! That's her! That's the car that was in the barn! That's his car! Quick, Sheriff, turn around, we've got to catch her."

For the first time since they'd met Vivien did not have to plead her case as the sheriff slowed the cruiser, cramped the wheel hard to the right, spun the car around in a half circle and gunned the engine. The cruiser roared and quickly picked up speed in pursuit. The sheriff radioed his dispatcher to let them know what was going on as Tom stirred in the back seat saying, "What is it?"

"It's Rachel," said Vivien, "she's trying to get away. Hold on, Tom."

"That bitch!" said Tom. "I knew it was her."

"Well, hold your horses, gang, we don't know nothing other than the fact that she or he or whoever is in that car is exceeding the speed limit and operating the vehicle in a reckless manner."

"Whatever," said Tom. "Just catch her and I'll bet she'll squeal."

A straight stretch in the road gave the sheriff the room he needed to feed the cruiser more gas. Vivien checked the tension of her shoulder strap and pushed her feet against the floor but she knew a crash at this speed would probably kill them all. She envisioned the car leaving the roadway, plunging over an embankment or hitting a tree. It probably wouldn't be a bad way to go but she wasn't ready. At the very least she wanted some answers to this mystery.

Vivien began calculating in her mind how far they could be from the bridge and what would happen when they got there. In the distance she caught a glimpse of the Mercedes' taillights and felt the sheriff stamp the accelerator to the floor.

She looked over and noticed his face had changed from kindly country lawman to a look of fierce concentration as he gazed forward into the distance. She checked the speedometer, noticed they were over a hundred miles an hour and tried to remember if she'd ever gone that fast in her life. Maybe once when she was on a date with a boy who liked to drag race on the country roads just beyond town.

The distance between them and the twinkling red lights beyond closed, then grew larger, then the lights disappeared as the cars worked their way around bends in the road. Vivien thought for fleeting seconds that she smelled tire rubber, and then engine oil, and then maybe radiator coolant and then the lights were gone. Everything was a blur, everything was happening too fast.

She couldn't take it all in and then they were at the top of the hill looking down towards the still semi-submerged bridge. The Mercedes was heading down the hill and showed no signs of slowing; in fact it seemed to be accelerating.

"Oh my god," said Vivien. "She'll never make it."

She looked over at the sheriff who had a death grip on the steering wheel and was not making any moves to show he was slowing down either.

"Sheriff, you're not going to follow her across are you?" she asked.

"Watch me," he said.

"Don't be a fool, we'll all be killed," said Tom.

Vivien gripped the door handle and wanted to hug her dog but it was too late. She watched in horror as the Mercedes went even faster as it approached the rushing water. It hit the edge of the river at full speed and then, miraculously, shot across the water. Huge walls of water were flung from its sides as it plunged in and then slid across the surface, moving across the gray expanse with the engine racing. The car reached the other side, fishtailed once towards a large oak tree, then righted itself and accelerated up the other side of the hill. It reached the top, and navigated a twist in the road as the taillights vanished in the darkness.

"Ha!" said the sheriff. "She hydroplaned it right across. Just like we're going to do. Hang on!"

Vivien sucked in her breath and braced for impact as the cruiser accelerated again, hurtled down the hill and straightened out into a line heading directly into the water.

The sheriff seemed to be suddenly enjoying himself immensely. He screamed "WaaaaHoooo!" as the big sedan plowed into the river, pushing into the moving stream of water. Vivien felt the forward progress of the car coming quickly to a stop as they were still a good ten yards from the other side.

The car then gathered a second wind, the engine screamed as the water they had displaced flowed back against the doors on both side, splashing over the hood. They made it a few more feet as the engine died, warning lights came on, and the sheriff hit the steering wheel with his open hand.

"Dammit."

Vivien instinctively reached for the door handle, trying to pop it open, and already knew it wouldn't work. Water was already seeping in through the bottom of the door.

"We have to get out of this car now, roll your windows down!" shouted Vivien, but it was too late. The engine had died and the electrical system had shorted out when water flooded into the engine compartment.

"Don't nobody panic," said the sheriff. "The water isn't that deep otherwise she would have never made it across."

Mooky was sitting up on the back seat, panting, as Vivien reached back to stroke her head. Meanwhile Tom had managed to get his door cracked open and he struggled to push it farther.

"I think I can get out," shouted Tom. "Give me something to break the glass and I'll bust the windows open from the outside!"

There was a shotgun mounted in between Vivien and the sheriff but what they really needed was a hammer, or one of those escape hatchets that Tom had used in his road rage incident.

Vivien reflected on the irony of that as she looked at the shotgun, contemplating whether it was heavy enough to break through the safety glass of the cruiser, and whether Tom might use it against them as soon as he had it in his hands. She assumed it was loaded and then noticed five shells strapped to the butt of the gun.

"Just stay put," said the sheriff, but then they all felt the car move as the running water collected against the side and pushed against the vehicle. A torrent was also now running underneath the car, gently lifting it from its mooring to the ground.

"The car's moving," yelled Vivien, "we have to get out. Give him the shotgun, Sheriff!"

Tom was now pushing the back door open with his feet, and against all odds getting the door open on the downward flowing side of the car.

The sheriff looked at Vivien, who pointed at the shotgun. Then he looked at Tom and pulled the keys out of the ignition.

He fumbled for a few seconds but then got the key to the shotgun, unlocked it and fed it to Tom in the back seat. Water was now collecting on the floor as Tom pushed the door open enough to squeeze out with the shotgun.

He held on to the side of the car as he approached Vivien's door, raised the gun and struck the glass. Vivien heard a thumping sound from the strike, but the glass did not break.

"Hit it again," Vivien yelled. "Aim for the dead center."

Tom did as he was told, and struck the glass again, which caused a crack to appear.

"One more time," said Vivien.

Tom hit it again and this time the window became a spiderweb of cracks and missing pieces. Vivien pivoted her hips and kicked at the glass which finally gave way. She pushed her feet through the hole, rotating her hips to get her butt through and feeling thankful for the five pounds she'd lost in the last year. She felt her legs react to the cold water as she pushed herself upright, holding on to the door for support.

"Come on, Sheriff, we'll pull you out!"

The sheriff began making his way across the front seat and looked at the open hole where the window used to be with obvious doubt.

"I'm not sure I can fit through there."

Vivien carefully moved to the rear of the halfway-submerged vehicle and began coaxing Mooky. "Come on girl, you need to get out of there, let's go!" Mooky ducked her head once, went into a hunched position and, being a black lab, leaped from the rear seat into the river in one fluid motion. The leap carried her beyond the car, beyond Vivien, as she was quickly caught up in the rushing current. Vivien's heart sunk as he she watched Mooky dog-paddling at full speed and heading downriver.

"Goddammit!" said Vivien as she slapped the roof of the car.

"What happened?" said Tom as he was trying to guide the sheriff's boot clad feet out the window.

"Mooky just jumped into the river! Jesus!" said Vivien.

"Oh shit," said Tom. "Help me get the sheriff out and we'll go find her next."

Vivien knew the priority was another human being, even though she felt like Tom could get the sheriff out and to the side of the river without her. She fought the urge to abandon them, and helped the sheriff get his feet, legs, hips and belly through the opening.

"Much obliged," he said as he made it to his feet. "Where's the dog?"

"She jumped out the door and the river took her downstream."

"Oh mercy," said the sheriff. "Let's hope she climbs out before she reaches the falls."

"The falls!" said Vivien. "Oh my god, how far are the falls?"

"Not that far," said the sheriff. "Come on, let's get to the bank and see if there's a way to follow the river. She's a smart dog, she'll probably swim to the edge and climb out on her own."

Chapter 22

Mooky was very excited to be in the water. Her head scanned from right to left looking for a thing to get. The thing could be a bird or a ball or a stick that Vivien had thrown for her, but she didn't see anything in front of her. She was moving very fast in the cold water and this also made her very excited. She was swimming as fast as she could run! Trees and bushes on the sides of the river were flashing by her as she went faster and faster. She was waiting to see a stick or a ball come flying into the river from behind her. She wanted to Get the Thing because this was the time of go.

Vivien had told her it was time to go and now she was, but she also realized she was going farther from Vivien the longer she stayed in the water looking for the thing. The smells of the car and Vivien were quickly disappearing behind her. The noise of the rushing water was drowning out the sounds of Vivien and the others trying to get out of the car. She could feel her legs and paws bouncing off rocks and sticks as she moved them around trying to find the bottom of the river.

She could hear a noise in front of her, a roaring noise off in the distance that was getting louder the longer she swam in the cold, dark water. She searched the side of the river for Vivien and sniffed the air but water kept washing over her nose making it hard to smell anything. From behind her she thought she heard Vivien calling and she tried to swing her head around but the water was pushing her faster and faster forward. A tree floated by her and she tried to swim towards it but she bounced off a rock and yelped from the pain. There was a large rock in the middle of the river and she was heading straight toward it. She heard Vivien call her again and kept trying to turn around but the water was too strong. She heard other voices calling her. Voices she didn't know that well. She wanted to go back towards the voices but the water wouldn't let her turn around.

She couldn't remember the last time she had eaten or got a treat but she was hungry now and wanted to stop swimming. She wanted to see Vivien and play Get the Thing. She looked in the water again to see if somebody had thrown something for her to get but there wasn't anything that she could see. No balls, no sticks, no birds, but the rock was getting closer. It was a big rock and she swam towards it.

The river pushed her hard into the rock and she yelped again as her feet clawed at it. The part of the rock that was under the water was slippery and her feet couldn't hold on. Her head was pushed under the water as she struggled to climb on the rock. She was under the water and could not breathe; it was dark and the water was trying to hold her down. She missed Vivien and wanted to see her. She didn't want to be in the water or play Get the Thing anymore.

She felt like she was going to sleep and she was very tired. Tired of swimming and trying to climb out of the water. Her nose was full of water and she was getting cold. She was going down and now her back paws were on the bottom of the river. Before she went to sleep she decided she would try once more to get out and dry off and look for Vivien and the thing to get.

She arched her back and then pushed against the bottom of the river very hard. She felt herself going up and now the river was helping to push her up and she felt her front paws on top of the rock that was dry. She clawed against it now her head was out of the water. She sneezed and scratched the rock with her claws and she felt her belly scrape against the edge of the rock. She stretched her neck and pulled with all her strength and now the top half of her was on the rock. She sneezed again and pulled the rest of herself out of the water.

She stood on the rock and shook the water off as she heard the voices now getting closer. She looked at her beautiful tail and wagged it as her ears shot up at the sounds of the voices. It was Vivien and other people calling her from somewhere on the side of the river.

She couldn't see them but she could hear them. She looked towards the voices and started to pant, excited because this was the time of go and soon she would see Vivien and finally get to eat. She shook more water from herself and licked her paw, which hurt from trying to climb up the rock.

She wagged her tail and raised her ears, listening for the voices coming towards her. The water was very loud now all around her. She sniffed at the water and took a quick drink as she thought about jumping back in. She shook again, feeling the water leave her coat. The voices were closer and she pointed her nose towards them, trying to find them. They were on the side of the river but she could not smell them. She barked to tell them that she was looking for them and to warn them about the noise of the water. A big stick was floating towards her and she crouched, looking at it, wondering if that was the thing to get. She barked at the stick and then she heard Vivien, closer, saying, "There she is. Oh my god she's on that rock in the middle of the river! Oh jeez…"

Mooky did not know what any of those words meant but she wagged her tail and looked to where the voices were coming from. She thought she saw something moving on the bank of the river and her ears shot up as she looked to where the sounds were coming from.

"Do not move, Mooky. You stay there. Oh jeez. How deep do you think that water is out there?"

"No way of telling," said another voice. "We need a rope or something, then maybe one of us can go out there and get her and then the other two can pull her back."

"How close is the falls?" said Vivien.

"Too close for comfort, that's for sure. I mean, we could try to wait it out. The longer we stay, the less water will be rolling through here."

"We can't do that, Sheriff, she could jump off that rock any second."

"She might be able to make the swim," said another voice.

"Yeah, well, she's not your dog though, is she, Tom?"

"I'm not trying to start something, I'm just saying, she swam out there —if you coaxed her and we were standing ready on the bank, as deep in as we can go, maybe she could get close enough so we could grab her."

"People die in this kind of water all the time," said the other voice.

Mooky wagged her tail and panted, stepping closer to the edge of the rock, trying to get closer to Vivien's voice.

"Stop, Mooky," said Vivien. "See that? She's already acting like she's going to jump in. Are you sure there's no rope in the cruiser, Sheriff? Maybe an extension cord or something we can use?"

"I looked twice, ma'am. Nothing."

It was hard to hear because the water was making so much noise but Mooky sensed that Vivien was coming to get her. She could see them all moving around on the riverbank but the shadows were making it hard to tell exactly what was happening. She heard somebody talk about holding on to a tree and how cold the water was. She didn't know what those words meant but she wanted to see Vivien and she knew if she jumped back in the water she would be carried farther away. She turned around on the rock, thought about lying down but then decided to remain standing so she could see better.

She heard Vivien say, "That's it, hold on to me but for God's sake, let me make sure I can feel the bottom with my feet."

She could now see a shadow coming towards the rock, walking slowly through the rushing water that was up to the shadow's knees. Sometimes the shadow would go in deeper, sinking to its waist. Mooky could see two other men closer to shore, holding hands and also standing in the water. Mooky wagged her tail and panted when she realized the shadow was Vivien, and she wanted to be with her now in the water. She crouched and looked towards her, preparing to jump.

"No," said Vivien. "You stay there and be a good girl, Mooky. I'm coming to get you but you need to stay. Stay. You hear me?"

Mooky knew what some of those words meant and she did not want to stay, she wanted to go and she wanted to go now. She crouched again and panted and then tried to get farther down the rock towards the rushing, gushing water.

"Don't you do it," said Vivien. "I'm going to get you, do not move."

She was much closer now but Mooky couldn't smell her. The water and the wind were pulling all the smells away but now she could see her face clearly in the moonlight.

Vivien was getting closer, moving slowly in the rushing water, and now she was holding her hand out, saying, "Come on girl, we need to get you off that rock, almost there, don't move…"

Mooky did not know what those words meant as she leaned forward, trying to smell Vivien's outstretched hand.

"All right Mooky, almost there. You stay right there. Be a good girl and do the right thing for once. We're almost ready to go." Mooky started to pant at the sound of the word "go." She dropped her head, hunched for a second and then leaped directly at Vivien. She felt herself crash into her as Vivien said, "Umph, okay I got her! I got her, I'm coming back!"

Mooky felt Vivien's arms around her, squeezing her, and she squirmed a bit. She was very happy and if she could have moved her beautiful tail it would be wagging. They slowly made their way back to the riverbank as the noise from the water grew softer, and now she could see Tom, the thing she was trying to catch, and the other man who drove the car. She smelled wet leather and perspiration and now she was on the ground, shaking and panting and running around between Vivien's legs. Everybody was petting her and hugging her and then they said it was time to go. Mooky also hoped that it was time to eat.

The sheriff's radio had miraculously survived the journey from the flooded car to the riverbank, and now everybody's cell phones were working. The sheriff summoned his deputy to come pick them up and they rode back towards the Inn. Along the way Vivien tried to focus her thoughts and, for once, think like a detective. She assembled all the suspects' faces in her mind and began to weigh everything that had happened, everything she had learned, and everything she assumed. A theory formed in her head but she still had no proof. By carefully weighing the facts and the evidence, there was only one possibility of who the killer could be.

The ride back seemed to be over in seconds and they arrived to a small army of fire trucks, ambulances, and police cars. Vivien assumed that every law enforcement officer in two counties were now on the premises or camped out in the driveway waiting for instructions. They walked into the house single file as the sheriff pointed them towards the dining room.

"I want you all to take a seat and relax," he said. "Nobody leaves this room, and I mean nobody, understood?"

The rest of the guests, except for Rachel, were already seated around the table. Vivien noticed a large deputy stationed by the back door of the kitchen, and two more standing on the back porch. Amy and Tom embraced as they entered the room, and Amy said, "Oh my god, are you shot?"

"She just nicked me. The crazy bitch finally got a chance to shoot somebody, except it was the wrong person, right Vivien?"

"Pipe down," said the sheriff as he motioned for an EMT to enter. "Take a look at his arm but don't give him any sedatives. We need everybody awake and coherent till we can get through this. Anybody got any coffee out here?"

A voice from the living room indicated he did and that he also had something he wanted the sheriff to look at.

The sheriff turned to exit the room, but then stopped and said, "Anybody else who tries to leave will be treated as a fleeing suspect, understand folks?" Some of the group nodded and murmured that they understood as the sheriff slid shut a pair of pocket doors that Vivien had not noticed before. Besides the EMT, the original group of suspects minus Rachel were all back in the same room again, but occupying different seats.

Lenny approached Vivien, lightly gripped her forearm and said, "What happened out there? Are you wet?"

"Mostly dry now but the car got stuck in the middle of the river. Mooky jumped out, almost drowned, and we saw Rachel driving away."

"You saw her?" asked Lenny.

"We saw the car, anyway. Somehow she hydroplaned it across the water, but when we tried to follow her the cruiser stalled in the middle of the bridge. Mooky jumped out and I had to go in after her."

"My god," said Lenny, "and you also shot Tom, is that true?"

"Yes, I thought he was going to hurt the dog. I'll tell you all about it later, but first I think I'm ready to solve the puzzle."

Vince snorted, Tom said, "Ow!" as the tech cleaned the wound, Wayne shifted his feet, and Svetlana appeared to be asleep with her head in her hands. Amy was watching the EMT treating her husband, like a hawk.

"Don't you think it's a little late, Vivien?" said Vince. "The cavalry has arrived so I think your sleuthing days are finally over, and I for one am relieved."

Vivien hadn't taken a seat as requested, and now she took half a step towards Vince.

"I don't believe you ever had a reason to fear, Vince, since you didn't kill him. But I have to admit I became suspicious when you started throwing your little temper tantrums."

"Oh really, Agatha?" he said. "And what makes you so sure it wasn't me? What was my big tell?"

"You kind of had a motive but not the temperament, Vince, as you are all bark and no bite. Even though you were rude to me I never considered you as a serious suspect, as you lack any kind of killer instinct."

Vince's eyebrows shot up as his bite was critiqued, but his face and sarcasm recovered quickly. "Well, praise Jesus," said Vince, "but you were convinced it was Tom, right? At least until Rachel disappeared."

"Actually no," said Vivien. "Although he didn't help his case by running out of the house, did he? He probably did think I was going to shoot him."

"And it turns out you did, didn't you?" said Tom, his voice dripping with malice from the other side of the room.

Vivien ignored him and turned back to Vince.

"Did you know our friend Tom here was involved in a road rage incident a few months ago – so he kind of has a history of violence, don't you Tom?"

"That was self-defense," Tom shot back as he stood up and the EMT pulled his hand away. "You can look that up too, lady, or maybe you missed that part."

"Oh I read the whole thing Tom, including the part where you killed the guy with the survival tool. Hatcheted him to death, right? Your relationships with women are also rather complicated too, but that's another matter, isn't it?"

"You can shut the fuck up, lady. Whatever you think you know about me is nobody's business."

"Agreed," said Vivien, "and also not related to what happened to Michael Samuels, but I am curious about where you got the gun, especially since your wife says you don't even like them – but at this point it doesn't matter, does it? I'm willing to bet yours was not the weapon used in the crime."

She turned on her heel, feeling more confident, and for some reason began thinking about *Perry Mason*, a lawyer show she'd watched as a kid on a black and white TV in the family living room back in Wisconsin.

"Anyway, if the police still think you're a suspect they'll check for powder burns on your hand, and the ballistics, and probably find nothing. If you'd fired the weapon you were pointing at me back at the river, that may have actually done you in. Luckily the dog distracted you, and I had the cooler head, so you will be exonerated. Bad temper, charming at times, probably a submissive male but not a murderer."

Vivien briefly considered that she may be stealing the sheriff's thunder, or even compromising the investigation, but she didn't care. She was determined to find out if she was right. Part of her was also convinced that the local authorities would not be able to bring the case to justice. She would never say that out loud, it would be rude and unprofessional, and so she plunged ahead.

"Which brings us to sweet little Dr. Amy, who is also not a killer even though she did have a motive."

"What motive?" said Amy with more than a trace of anger in her voice.

"The near assault in the barn," said Vivien. "Although I still think you may be holding back a few details, aren't you?"

"Details? What kind of details?"

"I saw the way he was looking at you, and the way you were reacting to him. I'm very curious about why you would even go in the barn in the middle of a thunderstorm to do, what, look at a horse? With your riding crop? Doesn't really add up, does it?"

"You know, you really should mind your own business, Vivien. I couldn't care less about what you think of me, or your flawed theories," said Amy.

Vivien shrugged and said, "Doesn't matter to me if there was something else in play between you two, but you, my dear, are also not the killer."

"Look, we all know who did it. It was Rachel," said Wayne. "That's why she ran off. Easy to see that."

Everybody turned to look at Wayne as looks of surprise crossed many of the group's faces. Vivien, on the other hand, was expecting some kind of reaction and now she had it.

Vivien did a half turn and faced Wayne. "That does make some sense, Wayne. She was with him the longest and probably had a million reasons to take a whack at him but I think she really did love him and therefore could not have killed him."

"She was cutting the phone lines to cover her trail for god's sake," said Wayne, his voice rising in volume. "She stole his car. What more proof do you need?"

Vivien knew she was close and hoped she could finish before the sheriff came in and ruined her fun.

"She loved him, Wayne. Love will make people do things they normally wouldn't do. I believed her when she said she didn't think he was actually dead and that she cut the phone lines to keep me from alerting the media. Part of her job was keeping his name out of the papers. She was Samuels' protector and lover. I get that part. Not sure why she stole the car, but that will be revealed eventually. Maybe she panicked, or just wanted to get out of here."

"And what about you, Vivien, or your odd little friend there? How do we know you're not the killer?" asked Wayne.

Lenny stiffened at being referred to as an "odd little friend," but Vivien held up her hand, imploring without a word that he should remain silent.

"Fair question, Wayne; except that Lenny is the only one amongst who was not verbally assaulted by Samuels."

"Not assaulted," said Lenny, "but still offended."

"Still not enough motive to make Lenny pull the trigger, Wayne. And even though he did threaten to shoot my dog, I, despite what you all think of me, still consider myself to be a rational, disciplined, peace officer."

"Who fucking shot me," said Tom.

"As you drew a weapon," said Vivien. "Which brings us to Svetlana."

"You leave her out of this," said Wayne as his voice evened out into a deadpan threat and his posture went ramrod straight.

"I can't, Wayne, because she holds the key to the mystery, don't you Svetlana?"

"I tell you what happened," said Svetlana as she raised her head and tilted her chip up.

"You did tell me – part of it anyway. Was the belt already around his neck when you ran out of the barn?"

"I tell you this already."

"Yes of course you did and you have no reason to lie, unless of course you risk being deported, as our friend Tom here suggested awhile back."

"Nobody's deporting anybody," yelled Wayne who was now out of his chair, his face starting to turn red. "Svetlana, you don't need to say another word. This is all a bunch of horseshit. Rachel did it, that's why she's gone. Any fool can see that."

"So it seems, Wayne, but there's still a few loose ends here, aren't there? Like how did the body get up in the hayloft, or better yet, who even knew there was a hayloft besides you, Wayne?"

"Every barn in this county has a hayloft, lady. Just because you city folks don't know nothing it doesn't mean it's not right."

"Okay, Wayne, every barn in the county has a hayloft and everybody knows that. Did Rachel carry him up there, or use the pulley to hoist him up there? I'm sure she's capable of many things but that would require a certain amount of upper body strength, and she didn't strike me as the gym rat type. Svetlana, on the other hand, looks like she's strong enough to hoist a body into the hayloft in an attempt to hide it."

"You shut the hell up, lady. I've had enough of this. She had nothing to do with it."

"If she didn't, Wayne, that only leaves one person who knew about the hayloft and had enough strength to hoist him up there. Why did you come out to the barn, Wayne? To check on the horse? Did you find Samuels and your Svetlana having sex in the barn, maybe with the belt around his neck? Was she maybe helping him out by pulling on it as she—?"

"They were not having sex, okay? He tried to rape her! He had his hands all over her and he already did have the belt around his neck, so yeah, fine. Give me the electric chair; I blew his damn brains out and would do it all over again!"

Amy gasped. Vivien tilted her head up in vindication. Tom held a bandage against his wound as his jaw dropped, and Lenny said, "Hmph," just as the sheriff slid the door open. He said, "All right folks, thanks for your patience. We're just going to get your statements and then we can all get some rest."

"Actually, Sheriff, that may not be necessary as Wayne here has just confessed," said Vince. "I have to admit, Viv, I didn't think you had it in you."

"Screw you, Vince," said Vivien with a smile.

Chapter 24

Two Months Later

Vivien opened the front door and felt a blast of cold air slide through her bathrobe. She instinctively reached to close the gap in the fabric as she cracked open the storm door and reached for the newspaper laying on the welcome mat on her front porch. It was the Sunday edition so it was heavier than the daily. As usual the ads in the blue wrapping tried to slide out from the center as she hefted it through the door while trying not to let all the heat out.

She had already read the article she was most interested in online, as it went live on *The Washington Post* website the day before. She had pored over the text, checking for accuracy and nervous about how she was being portrayed. She was also quite anxious about how the pictures had turned out, worrying about how she looked and how the house would appear to strangers. She grew up in a small town where everybody minded their own business and nobody wanted to be seen as trying to be better than anybody else, so she was of two minds about this whole thing.

On one hand, she didn't want her private life scattered all over town and was terrified about what people might think. On the other hand, it was all kind of exciting to see her own face looking back at her from the *Post* website.

She had already made the coffee and set out a plate of pizzelles which she found at the Polish deli in Rockville. Not quite as good as homemade but the thin, licorice-flavored cookies were still a favorite from childhood and she felt like she deserved a treat.

Mooky watched her from her spot in front of the back door in the kitchen, her tail gently thumping as Vivien came into the kitchen and laid the paper on the table.

"Here we go," said Vivien and began flipping through the sections. First she went to the Style section, but it wasn't there. She tried Metro, and again couldn't find it. Her heart sank as she embraced the possibility that it actually wasn't going to be in the paper after all.

She reviewed in her mind the phone interview with the reporter, and the day the photographer came out to take her picture. She'd already seen the story online so how could it not be in the paper? Maybe the reporter was wrong, or maybe she'd misunderstood. Maybe it was running next week.

She sighed heavily, took a bite of the cookie, lamenting that it was not quite chewy enough and figured it had to be a miscalculation in the dough, or maybe it was cooked a few seconds too long. For a moment her mind flashed back to a childhood memory of borrowing the special iron used to make the cookies from their neighbor, Mrs. Sostaric, who was Slovak and had all the right tools and the recipe. She remembered pouring the dough into the hot iron with her mother, who was not as interested in the process as Vivien but went through the motions to placate her daughter.

Vivien came back to the present and scanned the headlines on the top of the front page for the crisis of the day, then flipped it over and there it was, "Local Woman Solves Samuels Case."

"Oh my god, I'm on the front page!" said Vivien. "Mooky I'm on the front page." Mooky's tail thumped again at the mention of her name, and her ears perked slightly but her head did not change position on the floor. Vivien did a quick scan of the text to verify it was saying the same thing as the online version, then flipped the paper open and got up to fix coffee.

She came back with a steaming cup and once again read through the story about how she had cracked the case of the murder of Michael Samuels, who the *Post* called a "firebrand conservative media personality."

The article described how Vivien got Wayne to confess, and revealed that he had hidden the body and lied about the condition of the roads in order to keep everybody in the farmhouse while he hoped that somebody else would incriminate themselves – a plan that basically worked when Tom and then Rachel ran for the hills. If she had killed Tom, he may have gotten the blame.

The relationship between Wayne and Svetlana was never fully explained in the article, but everybody involved believed it went beyond employer and hired hand. Wayne's official confession revealed that he came into the barn as Samuels was trying to assault Svetlana. Wayne lost his temper, a fight ensued, Wayne got control of Samuels' gun and killed him using a horse blanket to deaden the sound of the shot. He initially hid the body in the horse stall, not counting on Mooky to get wind of the scent.

Wayne was afraid he'd be tried for murder, lose the farm and Svetlana, so he began trying to cover his tracks. The county District Attorney considered the case to be self-defense at best, and justifiable homicide at the worst. Wayne wasn't charged with anything.

The article also described the curious and ongoing tale of Rachel. A few weeks after her disappearance she was accused by Samuels' estate of stealing cash and stock certificates worth millions. The authorities found the white Mercedes in a long-term parking lot at the Cincinnati airport, where she had boarded a flight to New York and then booked a first-class ticket to Paris. After that, she vanished and remained missing.

The article described how Samuels mistrusted banks and kept much of his wealth in cash. Rachel, it seemed, knew where the cash was located and had the keys. His will was a complicated mess; vultures and leeches populated his family. There was another woman in the picture besides Rachel, and possibly some illegitimate children.

Vivien speed-read through to the end where the reporter asked about the future and how she felt about cracking the case. Vivien had rehearsed the answer in her head before she gave it, and had the reporter read the quote back to her before the interview ended.

The reporter had cleaned up the grammar but Vivien's thoughts were intact. She said, "Years of training as a police officer and an agent for the Secret Service prepared me for my one moment of fame. I was glad I could help local law enforcement. Maybe I should start a second career as a private detective."

She laughed after she said it and the reporter chuckled along with her, adding, "Hey, why not?"

Vivien exhaled a long breath and looked out her window: leaves were falling from the trees and blowing around in the autumn wind. The holidays were right around the corner, a time Vivien looked to with mixed emotions. Most of her family was dead or out of touch. She still had the dog, of course, a boyfriend who loved her, and Lenny, so maybe this year would be better. She folded the paper, and thought about framing the article as her cell phone and landline both rang at the same time.

Chapter 25

Mooky lay on the floor as the marvelous smell of coffee filled the room. The tiny draft of cold air blowing in from the back door carried smaller smells of leaves and dirt and the cat that lived up the street, but not enough to warrant a look. Vivien was talking on the phone and the other one was making noise at the same time. Mooky thumped her beautiful tail against the floor, anticipating visitors.

Usually after the phones rang it was time to go in the car and see the other dogs at the park. Sometimes people would come to the house after the noise stopped, so she was already on guard. They might play with her or pat her head or give her a treat if she was a good girl.

They might all go outside to play Get the Thing, of if not, Mooky would spend some time looking for squirrels or sniffing for the other animals that came out at night. It was not time to eat yet and the sun was shining down on her through the window, warming her coat. Vivien hadn't made any mention of going out but Mooky knew if she lay here long enough that sooner or later it would be the time of go and this was the greatest time of all.